THE GREAT MYSTERY OF ETERNITY

JAMIE MCNABB

COPYRIGHT NOTICES

Copyright 2020 by Jamie McNabb

Cover Graphic: La barca de Caront, Josep Benlliure Gil, Museu de Belles Arts de València

All rights reserved

Published by Soapbox Rising Press

ISBN: 978-1-948447-09-6

This book is licensed for your personal enjoyment only. All right reserved. This is a work of fiction. Any similarity to actual persons, events, or locations is purely coincidental. This book or any party thereof may not be reproduced in any form without permission.

DEDICATION

For Marie and S/V *Magic Margin*

Table of Contents

Acknowledgements..vii

Introduction... 1

Crossing the Acheron....................................3

The Muzzle Flash...21

Fr. Andrei Meets Comrade Stalin................45

The Bank Teller..61

The Rabbi, the Vampire, and the Mitzvot...87

The Cormorant..117

Three Guys and a Bar.................................139

The Second Mate's Cup of Tea..................165

Marina Dogfish Chow................................187

The /Mooring Buoy....................................217

Review and Contact...................................231

About the Author..233

ACKNOWLEDGMENTS

If it had not been for the tireless efforts of the copyeditors, publishers, short-order cooks, coffee roasters, chiropractors, friends, and psychotherapists involved, this humble project would never have been completed.

Above all, there never would have been a project in the first place without the dedication and highly skilled efforts of Alec Wilson. He voiced the audio version, and he patiently kept this collection from growing into a scatter-shot behemoth. And, too, half in jest and half in earnest, he named it.

Thanks to one and all!

INTRODUCTION

This introduction provides a brief sketch of The Great Mystery of Eternity. A note on terminology: collections are drawn from the work of a single author, whereas anthologies are drawn from the works of several different authors. Yes, I know, it's a lot of marketing jargon, but it can make a lot of difference. For one thing, as far as anyone can tell, Eternity is not arbitrary.

THIS IS A COLLECTION of short stories. Some are as seasoned as the best Scotch whiskey; some are as new to the world as salmon smolt. The genres vary, but in one way or another, they are bound together by the great mystery of Eternity. Or aspects of it. Or everyday reflections of it, if only in the minds of the characters. Overtly or covertly.

A word of caution. This collection is eclectic. There are sea stories, religious stories, adventure stories, historical stories, two first-contact stories, and so on. Such groupings are, after all, somewhat arbitraries, and any given story might fall into more than one group. Or it may fall between groups.

Leave the so-called rules behind, and enjoy the ride.

As always, your comments, suggestions, and questions are welcome.

CROSSING THE ACHERON

Between death and Eternity stands the ferryman. No money, no ticket. No ticket, no passage. No passage, no entry into Eternity. No entry into Eternity ... well, that option doesn't bear thinking about.

THE NEWBIE PATTED DOWN his pockets. His wallet was gone, his money clip was gone, and even his parking-meter feed was gone. "I'm sorry," he said to the toll collector. "I don't have any money."

The toll collector sat in a booth at the top of the ramp leading down to the ferry dock. He was dressed in a white robe and wore a helmet with silver wings. "Did you arrive with anything of value?"

The ferry was alongside, and the ferryman was bullying a fresh load of passengers into their places. "You! Yes, on *that* thwart. Yes, the benchlike board! Will you never learn? Oh, what I wouldn't give for a few right seaman!"

"Value?" Basil asked. "No, I don't think so."

The toll collector's face took on a suspicious expression, as though the newbie were trying to deceive him. "No coin? Not even one? Under your tongue perhaps?"

The newbie, who'd begun and ended his life as Basil Wainwright, hadn't thought of that. He poked his tongue into the various corners of his mouth. Empty. "No, nothing."

A sharp sense of urgency sniggled through Basil's gut. Weren't they going to let him across? It wasn't his fault they'd buried him without any money.

"Coins can be very small," the toll collector said. "Perhaps you swallowed it."

Basil was sure he hadn't. He would have remembered swallowing a coin. "I don't think so."

"No!" the ferryman bellowed. "We have no cabins!"

The ferryman wore a short, mottled brown tunic. His beard, which was unkempt and gray, hung to the middle of his chest.

"What did you say?" a tremulous male voice asked from the middle of the boat. "I didn't hear."

"No! Cabins! Are you deaf as well as dead?"

"Yes, I am. Deaf. *Was* deaf, I guess you'd say. I don't know what I am now."

"Hold on!" Basil said. He checked his left hand, but his wedding ring was gone. "Shit! She must have kept it." Then he noticed he was wearing his watch. She mustn't have had a use for it, or maybe her good-for-nothing brother hadn't wanted it. Basil showed it to the toll collector. "How about this?"

"Watches don't mean a lot here. We're on the border of Eternity, you see."

Basil's heart sank, which, in a way, was what had landed him here in the first place. He stared at his watch. No meaning? How could that be? After all, the second hand was jumping from mark to mark. "But my watch is working," he said. "The ferryman—"

"Charon's his name," the toll collector said.

"Charon," Basil repeated. "Thanks. Yes, well, anyway, Charon could use it to time his crossings, establish a schedule, and so forth."

"Schedules mean even less than watches. No time, you see, not in the conventional sense."

CROSSING THE ACHERON

"But I can feel it passing."

"You only imagine you can," the toll collector said. "It's all part of the Great Mystery of Eternity."

Charon climbed aboard and worked his way to the stern.

Basil was suddenly gripped by an urge to run down and jump aboard the ferry, to fight his way onto it if need be.

He looked on in horror as the boat's mooring lines were cast off.

Charon sculled a few yards away from the dock and harangued his charges through running out their oars.

Horrified or not, Basil found the process of getting the ferry under way fascinating, so fascinating that it overshadowed his sense of abandonment.

"Sir?" the toll collector prompted impatiently. "Step aside, sir, if you please."

"But I do *not* please," Basil said. "I have to cross the river."

Finally, the rowers and their oars were ready. "All right, you lubbers! Together now. Give way!" The sound of Charon's voice boiled up the riverbank. "Stroke!" The oars dipped into the water and pulled aft. The ferry glided forward.

The toll collector jutted his chin in the direction of the fields behind Basil. "They all feel exactly the same way you do, but they won't get across unless they pay the toll."

Basil hadn't taken much notice of the fields before, but now he gave them a careful look. They flanked the line that ran down from the Valley of the Shadow to the toll booth. The fields were covered with grass, dotted with oak trees, and sprinkled with flowers. The whole was blanketed in patches by those who couldn't cross, by those who'd arrived without a coin or similar object of value.

Here and there, lights strobed. They made the place look like an enormous picnic attended by people who'd forgotten to turn off the flashes on their cameras.

"There must be millions of us," Basil said.

"Billions."

The toll collector's apparent indifference was staggering. Basil said, "*Billions* of us can't be left to mill around between life and death forever!"

"No, you can't. Which is why, if you stay on this side long enough, you'll wink out of existence."

Basil felt his legs go rubbery. "What?"

"See those bursts of light? They're what happen when someone winks out." The toll collector smiled admiringly. "I'm told it's a dandy way to go."

"You're insane!"

"Granted, it sounds harsh, but you said it yourself: everything has to be in one state or the other. You can't be left in between."

"Now, sir, I need you to move along. You're holding up the line. Next!"

An old woman in a green suit and pearl necklace elbowed Basil aside. Ever the gentleman, he mumbled, "Sorry. Excuse me," and stepped farther out of her way.

She made no acknowledgement, but took his place at the front of the line.

Furious at her, and at himself, and at his wife, and at the toll collector, Basil put a few more paces between himself and the tollbooth. From there, he watched the old woman, curious to find out whether or not her luck would be any better than his had been.

The old woman and the toll collector went through the business about coins and watches, and then she took off her pearls

CROSSING THE ACHERON

and handed them over.

"Very nice," the toll collector said. He put the pearls in an iron-bound chest and handed the woman a boarding pass. "Enjoy your crossing."

Basil moved farther off.

The ferry, now in midstream, was a double-ender. It was longer than an old-fashioned lifeboat, but about as wide.

"You there, forward!" Charon yelled. "Yes, you! Row dry!"

Charon eased his steering oar to starboard and the boat swung to port, clearing a piece of driftwood.

~~*

Basil went and stood under one of the oak trees a dozen yards up from the river. A man was sitting there, his back to the tree trunk. He was middle-aged, had a neatly trimmed beard, and was wearing a black frock coat.

The man looked up. "Cancer. How about you?"

It took Basil a second to catch up. "Heart attack."

"Too bad," the man said. "Take a load off."

Basil sat down.

The man held out his hand, "George Odysseus Taylor."

After the introductions were out of the way, George said, "You've met Mercury."

"Come again?"

"The fellow in the tollbooth."

"Yes, I've met him." Further comment seemed pointless.

George shrugged. "Well, what are you going to do?" He pointed at the river. "Not much to look at, is it?"

"The Styx?"

THE GREAT MYSTERY OF ETERNITY

"The Acheron."

"Sorry." It was more of a question than an apology.

George laughed. "Don't fret yourself. Almost everyone confuses them. The Styx is miles away."

As for the Acheron, Basil couldn't think what he ought to have expected, but a sluggish, narrow stream wasn't it.

This sparked an unsettling question. "I'm not comatose, am I?" Basil asked.

"No, you're dead, all right. Mind you, we're not completely dead, not yet. We have to cross the river."

"To enter the afterlife itself?" Basil asked.

"That's right. It happens just beyond that ridge on the other side."

Hoping for the merest hint of an explanation, Basil asked, "How did I get mixed up in a Greco-Roman myth? I'm a Congregationalist."

"I'm an atheist," George said. "Imagine my surprise."

"Ha, ha, ha," Basil said, letting his sarcasm off its leash. "I suppose it's all part of the Great Mystery of Eternity."

"Mercury couldn't have said—"

A light strobed thirty paces away. A split second later, a scream followed, and then hysterical sobbing.

"What happened?" Basil asked. Then realizing what had happened, he asked, "Who was it?"

The sobbing rose to a wail, then subsided into a dull keening.

George stood, looked hard in the direction from which the flash had come, and sat back down.

"The woman crying is Molly Sheraton, twenty-five, automobile wreck. The person who winked out must have been Bob Lewis, thirty-one, fisherman, drowned at sea," George said.

CROSSING THE ACHERON

"They were close."

The sobbing quieted, and Basil saw a knot of women walking uphill, away from the Acheron. The woman in the middle had her face buried in her hands.

Desperation threatened to swamp Basil.

"How long do we get?" he asked.

"Winking is random. Could be hours, could be millennia. One instant you *are*, and the next instant you are *not*."

A few minutes later, Basil made his excuses and walked down to the water's edge.

Charon had discharged his passengers and was sculling back. His face was grim. Back and forth, back and forth—he had to be bored out of his mind.

Basil considered the Acheron. It couldn't be more than two hundred yards across. Maybe as little as a hundred and a half.

A plan hatched.

Basil waded into the river. The bottom was sand—fine, white grains, the sort that came in egg timers. The first few yards were easy, but then the bottom dropped away. He pushed off and swam.

The landscape on the other side was similar to the one behind him: rolling hills, trees, flowers. The hills rose up to form the ridge George had pointed out. No one was around.

Never a good swimmer, Basil quickly tired. He rolled onto his back. He could see George is the distance, sitting under their oak tree.

When Basil crossed what he took to be the middle of the river, he heard a dog barking from ahead. It had to be Cerberus.

Basil swung around to have a look.

Cerberus was a yellow Lab. He was pacing back and forth at the edge of the water and barking his head off, not a threatening bark, but the bark of a dog who wants to play.

A happy yellow Lab—another surprise in what was turning out to be a surprising ... eternity.

Deciding to cross that canine bridge when he came to it, Basil rolled onto his back and settled into a gentle kick-drift motion. He gazed up into the vault: no rock ceiling, but a blue sky with high white clouds.

George and the oak tree were still in position behind him.

Basil's head hit something hard. Startled, he bolted upright in the water. He'd run into a log. He worked his way around it, checked his course, and took up where he'd left off.

The dog stopped barking.

It was going to work! So much for Mercury and his demand for a coin!

Basil touched bottom, stood, and turned around.

George came forward and offered him a towel. "Here, let me help you out of those wet clothes."

"What are you doing over here?" Basil asked. "How did you get across?"

"I didn't."

Basil jerked his head around, searching back the way he had come. George had to be lying! But he wasn't. There on the opposite bank was the guardian hound of Hades, smack on the beach where Basil had *thought* he had landed.

Basil's jaw clenched and his eyes burned.

Annihilation. It seemed inevitable now.

He blinked back his tears. He had to keep his emotions in check. Panic would solve nothing.

"You might have warned me about the river," Basil said, and tugged off his sodden jacket.

CROSSING THE ACHERON

"New arrivals are a lot like babies," George said. "Most of what they need to learn, they have to teach themselves."

Basil sat down under the tree and took off his shoes. Another thought occurred. He looked up and down the river.

"Don't bother," George said. "No matter how far you go, no matter which direction you take, this is where you'll end up."

~~*

After Basil's clothes had dried, he went to have a talk with Mercury, the toll collector.

Mercury said, "You have to cross in a ferry. The Acheron itself turned you back."

"But how?"

"It's all part of the Great Mystery of Eternity."

~~*

Basil dropped onto the ground under the oak tree. He hugged his legs. Desperation wasn't like him, but then again, neither was being sort of dead.

"How'd it go?" George asked.

"What am I supposed to do?" Basil asked. "What are *we* supposed to do?"

"If any of us had an answer to that one, we'd have used it, don't you think?"

Basil did think. To cross the Acheron, a ferry had to be taken. To ride Charon's ferry, the toll had to be paid. This raised another question. "What do they do with the tolls?"

"Nothing. They're sitting in a strong room under the tollbooth." George made one of those incredulous expressions, the sort popular when frock coats were popular. "Forget about it. You wouldn't care for what they did to you once they caught up to you, which they would."

Scratch that, then. Basil wanted to cross the Acheron, not anger the powers that be.

"Apropos of tolls," George said, "people are sent here with just about anything you can imagine: weapons, tools, toys, books, religious items, wives, husbands, pets—the whole gamut. But Mercury and Charon are only interested in coins and jewels."

"I'd accept whatever I was offered," Basil said.

"What an original thought," George said, letting his own sarcasm show.

Out on the river, Charon was about halfway across. The sight of his loaded ferry was like a knife in Basil's heart.

Suddenly, an idea fell into place. "You said tools. What kind of tools?"

"All kinds. Their owners figure that sooner or later Charon will accept them in payment. He won't, but those tools are their only hope."

Basil stood. "Their only hope? No, they're not."

"What are you talking about?"

"I'm going to go have a talk with Charon. You go down to the river and haul ashore as many logs as you can."

~~*

Charon gazed at Basil as though he were a patch of dry rot. "Where's your boarding pass?"

"I don't have one," Basil said.

"Then what're you doing here?"

The first passenger for the impending trip toddled across the dock and climbed into the boat.

"Where shall I sit?" she asked.

"On a bench," Charon snarled. To Basil, he said, "That one's as dumb as a retarded ox."

"Which is why I'm here," Basil said. "I think you could use a deck hand."

"Maybe, but I can't use you."

"Are you sure?"

"I know your type," Charon said. "You just want to learn the trade so you can chisel me out of my business." He picked up an oar. "Get off my dock!"

~~*

When he returned, Basil found George and half dozen men and women wrestling a log onto the beach. The newcomers told him how happy they were to have work to do, and they asked him why he wanted the wood. Their faces were alight with purpose.

Basil waded into the water and joined them.

As soon as they'd beached the log, Basil asked, "Who brought tools?"

No one had. They were eternity's destitute.

"No matter. Whatever else we'll need, we'll need wood."

Basil didn't tell them that without money they'd have no use for either the tools or the wood.

~~*

THE GREAT MYSTERY OF ETERNITY

Charon made four more round trips before he left his boat and strode up to Basil.

Charon asked, "How much do you want me to pay you?"

Basil had his answer ready. "One coin for every round trip."

"Fair enough."

"And I want two days out of every seven off."

"I don't get days off!" Charon said.

"Not my problem," Basil said.

"How do we measure the days?"

"My watch has a calendar function."

"You're a clever one." Charon stabbed a finger at Basil. "I'm telling Mercury that he's not to sell you a ticket under any circumstances."

"But I get my time off, right?" he said.

"Right."

"One last detail," Basil said. "As long as I'm working for you, I don't suddenly disappear."

"Not my call," Charon said, "but I'll put in a good word for you with upper management."

"Fair enough," Basil said.

~~*

By the end of Basil's second week on the ferry, the gang on the beach had grown to two dozen and a respectable pile of logs and branches lay on the grass.

Seated under the oak tree, Basil gave George his bag of coins. "Buy some tools, saws in particular. It's time we got started on the shipway."

"Shipway?"

CROSSING THE ACHERON

"The bedlogs upon which we'll lay the new ferry's keel."

~~*

They spent the rest of the weekend trading coins for saws and other tools, figuring out how to cut their logs into bedlogs, and sorting the branches into types: long, straight pieces for oars and curved pieces for ribs.

On what Basil defined as Monday morning, Charon said, "It's a long way from a pile of wood to a working ferry, but you're welcome to try."

Basil wasn't sure he'd heard right. Charon's tone had bordered on the encouraging. "My wife and I built a house once," Basil said. "None of it went the way we'd planned, but in the end, we had a house." Basil felt tears on his cheeks and wiped them away.

Charon said, "It's no good being stuck on this river. You're dead and you're alone, no matter how many friends you make." He added, "Every trip, you watch 'em scramble ashore, their faces burning with excitement."

"Where do I sit?" a man asked. He had a New England accent and was dressed in what might have been his best tweeds.

Charon's face flashed with contempt. "At an oar!"

Unperturbed, the man nodded and took a place in the bow.

To Basil, Charon said, "Today, I'll teach you how to scull. Tomorrow, we'll work on steering."

~~*

That weekend, Basil, George, and their gang, now three dozen strong, landed a straight, stout log they decided would make a good keel. They squared it and set it in place on the bedlogs. They cheered and took the time to imagine what the finished boat would look like.

~~*

Several weeks later, on a Wednesday, Basil arrived at the ferry late. As he walked onto the dock, part of the day's first load was already taking their places.

Charon yelled something at him in Greek, and Basil got down to business. He showed the passengers what to do and when to do it. The instant he'd finished, they were all eyes for the other side, pointing and laughing.

"How's your boat progressing?" Charon asked.

"We're gaining on it," Basil said. "Dozens of unexpected details. You know how it is."

"Indeed, I do."

The last of the load straggled down from the tollbooth, a woman in heels and a man in a military uniform. There was nothing odd about that, but what did strike him as odd was the fact that they were two passengers short.

Just then, Mercury jogged down onto the dock. His face was flushed, and he'd forgotten to bring his helmet.

"I'm not late, am I?" he asked, and climbed aboard.

"What are you doing here?" Basil asked.

Mercury shrugged. "It's all part of the Great Mystery of Eternity."

"That's not an answer," Basil said.

"Let him be," Charon said. "Every once in a while, Mercury

CROSSING THE ACHERON

makes the crossing. Gets him out of the booth, you see."

And it did make a certain amount of sense. Basil had his days off, and he couldn't see why Mercury shouldn't take one now and then. But why spend any of it rowing back and forth?

Mercury took one of the empty places.

Charon pushed the handle of the steering oar toward Basil. "Here," Charon said. "I've taught you almost everything you need to know. It's your turn now. Take us across."

"Aye, aye," Basil said.

Taking the last empty seat, Charon said, "I think I'll try rowing for a change."

Basil cast off the mooring lines, and went to his place in the stern. He settled his grip on the handle of the steering oar, and sculled the ferry away from the dock.

"Ready," Basil said. "Together, now. Give way!"

The oars swung forward, slipped into the water, and pulled aft. The boat moved forward. It had begun reasonably enough, but already there were crossed oars.

"Avast rowing!" Basil yelled. "You, there, in the blazer!"

"What?" a frantic male voice replied. "What have I done?"

"You've fouled your oar!"

"I don't understand."

"Are you blind as well as dead? You've fouled your oar. Clear it!"

The man uncrossed his oar.

"Together, remember. Wait for it. Ready. Give way! Better. Stroke! Row dry. Stroke! You there, stay in time. Stroke. Watch your oar. Stroke!"

By the time Basil's passengers understood that they were in fact expected to row in unison, the ferry was across the river.

Basil cajoled them through boating their oars, while he sculled the ferry up to the dock. He stepped out, made the boat fast, and released his charges.

They hurried up the slope. Only one or two turned back for a last look at the river and the shore they'd come from: the grassy hills, the oak trees, and the sporadic flashes.

Charon clapped Basil on the shoulder. "Well done, lad. It's time for your final lesson."

Mercury walked up the slope a few paces.

"What is it?" Basil asked.

Charon smiled. There was true joy in it, but also a hint of sadness. "The ferry's yours."

Cold spilled into Basil's feet and a pain unlike anything he'd ever experienced ripped into his chest like the talons of a raptor. "No!" Basil was sure he'd shouted, but he knew he'd only whispered. "No! I don't want it."

"Neither did I," Charon said. "I was Admiral Sir Nigel Albert Winfield Sumner back then. 1826, fever in Jamaica."

Mercury paused and looked back toward the dock. He beckoned.

"I don't care who you were," Basil said.

"I do. I'm finally Nigel again."

"I won't do it. I have to cross to the other side."

Nigel made a show of surveying their surroundings. "As far as I can tell, here you are, on the other side."

"But I—"

"Good-bye, lad. Take care of the boat. Don't worry about annihilation. Now that you're me, who I was, it won't happen. Same goes for your Mercury."

Nigel whistled and Cerberus bounded over to him.

CROSSING THE ACHERON

Nigel and the dog joined the man from the tollbooth, and then the three of them walked up and over the ridge.

A moment or two later, three hearty cheers sounded from beyond it.

The echoes faded, and Basil was completely alone.

For the first time since his arrival, he was free to make whatever choice he wished. There was no one to turn him away, no dog to set up an alarm, no friend to tell him what he could or could not do. Ahead of him, beyond the ridge, were his mother and father, aunts, uncles, and grandparents ... and friends who'd died before he had. He could find them, and then, surely, the ache that had plagued him for the last quarter of his life would end.

Behind him, beyond the Acheron, were the throngs of new arrivals, the masses of dead who couldn't pay the toll—the flashes and the half-built ferry, the ferry that Basil had conceived as a means to cheat his way across.

Basil ran up the slope.

His mother, his father, his friends, his family—he'd be with them soon. Very soon. He had nothing to do but cross that final ridge. Nothing to do but join them.

As he ran, his hands began to itch. Of themselves, they yearned for the touch of the ferry's steering oar.

~~*

George met him on the dock below the tollbooth. George was carrying the winged helmet.

"Where are Charon and Mercury?" George asked.

"They made the crossing," Basil said.

THE GREAT MYSTERY OF ETERNITY

"So that's how it is."

"Yep."

"I'm not surprised. How many of them have there been?"

"How many Indras have there been?" Basil asked.

"Who?"

"Never mind."

Touching the helmet, George said, "It fits, but I don't think I'll wear it, not with my frock coat. Too much eccentricity is bad for business."

"You're staying?"

"I like working."

The new Charon said, "We'll need a dog. Any around?"

"There's a guy with a Sheltie. Package deal, I'd say."

"Fine. The dog can be the new Cerberus, and the guy can keep the docks in order."

"What do we charge?" the new Mercury asked.

"A coin, if they have one, but we'll take whatever they offer. No more winkings out. We have boats to build."

The happiness faded from Mercury's face. "I saw you running toward the ridge. Why'd you come back?"

"I'm not sure," Charon said. "As your predecessor might have put it, it's all part of the Great Mystery of Eternity."

"That's not much of an answer," Mercury said.

"It's the best I can do. I must be stupid as well as dead."

THE MUZZLE FLASH

Bethany Chang knows she's about to die. How does she know this? Well, flying through the air gives her one pretty good clue. So do the fact that her clothes and hair are giving off an unmistakably singed smell. So lovely. Below her, the night-dark waters of the Strait of Georgia in British Columbia are waiting eagerly to enfold her in their chill embrace.

BETHANY CHANG knew she had at most only a few seconds to live.

She could have counted them on the fingers of one hand if she hadn't been flailing with both of her hands in the air. And her legs. For what little good it was doing her.

There had been the smell of propane, and a flash, and then an explosion. An explosion? Yes, an explosion. It had ripped through her sailboat, an Islander 32, affectionately named *Kerfuffle*. Sailing alone, Bethany had been bound from Vancouver, British Columbia, across the Strait of Georgia to Nanaimo, on Vancouver Island. They'd just barely reached the halfway point.

Bethany had been in the cockpit, steering, and Rajiv had been below, making coffee. No, that wasn't right. He hadn't been aboard. But if he had been, and if it had been the propane stove that had gone up, then it would have exploded right in front of him. He was, after all, always and forever making coffee, cup after cup. He said he liked it better than tea, but she found that hard to believe.

Anyway, if he had been aboard, which he hadn't, and if he had been making coffee, which he also hadn't, then he might have survived. But Bethany doubted it. Like as not, he would have ended up so much charred meat on the opposite side of the salon.

It was odd, damned odd, that she wasn't more distraught over the whole thing, being blown up and all. Maybe she hadn't had time to absorb what had happened, what was happening.

That had to be it.

Not enough time.

Not enough time to sort out what had happened.

She had been too busy.

Yes, that was it.

For example, at the moment, she was too busy performing her own inimitable impression of Mary Martin in *Peter Pan*, only without the wires ... or the fairy dust.

Not counting the propane.

Propane and fairy dust: they could both make you fly.

The primary explosion, or perhaps a secondary detonation from near the engine, a rebuilt Atomic 4, had thrown Bethany into the air.

She was travelling in a high arc, flying like a mortar shell.

Flying, flying, flying.

Miraculously, the explosion hadn't broken her legs, hadn't driven her leg bones out through her thighs, and hadn't shattered her spine. Instead, and this was the real miracle, it had thrown her clear of the boat. There'd be no coming back down onto a handy lifeline stanchion. Which was a good thing, a very good thing indeed.

Bethany would, however, land in the regrettably cold February waters of the Strait of Georgia. She was more likely to die from hypothermia than she was from drowning.

THE MUZZLE FLASH

Her situation was rather clear. Very little room for doubt. Almost none at all.

What she did not know was *why*. Why had someone rigged *Kerfuffle* to blow up? It didn't make any sense. Rajiv's parents, Jinhai and Mingzhu Chang, detested her, but they detested all Occidentals, especially anyone of British extraction. Besides, their beloved son, Rajiv, her husband, had been aboard, too. Therefore, it couldn't have been them.

But, no, that wasn't right.

Rajiv had *not* been aboard.

She'd been the only one on the boat.

The water below her, far below her, was very gray.

Her in-laws were very polite about their attitudes toward her. They never called her a "red-haired monkey" or a "round-eyed gold digger" or a "lazy, blonde Gweilo" or a "running dog of European cultural imperialism" to her face. They were very Canadian in that regard. Always careful to avoid giving overt offense. Plenty of smiles and hot tea. Or coffee, as the occasion dictated. Mostly tea.

Bethany didn't like knowing that that was how they felt about her, and she especially didn't like the emotions toward them that it sparked within her, but there the whole interracial mess was. Like it or not.

Maybe she could bring them around.

The "round-eyed gold digger" charge made absolutely no sense. She had money of her own. Inherited, true, but hers. Not old money, but hoary enough. Lumber money from way, way back.

Anyway, given Jinhai and Mingzhu's utter loathing for people of British extraction, why had they chosen to immigrate to

Canada? Perhaps they couldn't get into the United States. Or perhaps their hatred for Occidentals had developed only after they'd settled in Vancouver.

Why they had named their son Rajiv, a decidedly Indian name, was another one of the many mysteries that populated Bethany's life.

Her feet rotated above her, and for a brief moment she was upside down.

Broken neck, anyone?

She figured that given everything that was happening to her, she wasn't going to live long enough to find out any of the answers to any of her questions.

Just then she saw a bright, elongated flash of red and white.

One of their kayaks had been thrown out of its bracket and into the water. It was bobbing around like a crab-pot buoy. The explosion must have snapped the tie-down strap.

Suddenly, Bethany was in the water, which was even colder than she'd imagined it would be.

Down, down, entirely covered by the water, rolling, struggling, kicking, clawing at the water, thick and cold, clawing like a tiger, and then up and up and up, her head breaking free.

Taking in great lungfuls of air.

It felt nearly as cold as the water.

Her self-inflating life jacket opened. It's air chambers held her head out of the water. They were bright yellow. What a marvelous idea. Visibility. Good work, that engineer!

And with that generous thought in her mind and with the taste of saltwater in her mouth, Bethany passed out.

~~*

THE MUZZLE FLASH

A gentle thumping on the side of her head brought her around.

Regaining consciousness was a thoroughly unexpected, but also a thoroughly welcome, event.

Apart from the cold.

Apart from the thumping, which had grown tiresome.

It was the bow of the kayak, her kayak. Rajiv's was blue and white.

She shoved it away, but then realization dawned and she made a grab for it, catching it by the lifting handle.

"Nice kayak," she said through chattering teeth. "Come to mama. There's a good girl."

How she and the kayak had ended up in the same patch of water was another mystery, but Bethany wasn't about to question it.

She looked around and spotted *Kerfuffle* several dozen meters away. Without anyone at the tiller, the boat had rounded up into the wind. She was luffing viciously, but she was staying put. Sort of. She was drifting off to leeward, to the southeast, but then they all were, Bethany, *Kerfuffle*, and the kayak. Albeit at different rates.

A thin trail of smoke was rising from the companionway. The wind was carrying it off to leeward.

Bethany mustn't have been unconscious for very long, because *Kerfuffle* hadn't made it very far, and the kayak certainly would have, had it been given half a chance.

She had to get back aboard.

To do that, however, given the distances and the water temperature, she'd have to climb aboard her kayak and paddle over to *Kerfuffle*.

She and Rajiv had practiced the maneuver several times. In warm water, or in what was accepted as warm water in British Columbia.

THE GREAT MYSTERY OF ETERNITY

The maneuver was simple enough. All she had to do was make like a seal hauling itself up onto a navigation buoy for a nice snooze in the sunshine.

Easy.

Not.

By the time Bethany had flopped aboard, she'd nearly rolled the kayak over on top of herself three times. But the fourth had done the trick.

She began paddling.

~~*

The after end of *Kerfuffle*'s cockpit didn't look too bad, but the forward end was a tangle of shattered fiberglass, wood, metal, hoses, and wires.

It reminded Bethany of the time that she and her sister, Corliss, known to one and all as Lizzy, had gone down to the States and bought "Indian fireworks" on one of the reservations. They'd then spent a blissful July afternoon on a beach shooting them off. The rockets had been fun, but the most fun had been using large firecrackers to blow things up: coffee cans, plastic jugs, wine bottles, and pop cans, mostly.

Bethany picked her way forward, moving carefully.

There was the heavy, sharp odor of raw gasoline.

The top of the engine was clearly visible: the block, the sparkplugs, the hoses, the wires, and the control cables. Beneath the engine, spilled gasoline was puddling in the bilges.

She could, or thought she could, hear a small but decided trickle.

The smoking lamp was definitely out.

THE MUZZLE FLASH

Not that she smoked.

That was Rajiv's vice.

The after end of the coachroof looked as though it had been ripped up and peeled forward. To port, over the stove, the side of the cabin had been reduced to a gaping hole surrounded by shredded fiberglass and splintered wood.

The mainsail boom looked like an aluminum soda straw that had been bent in half. The vang, which on *Kerfuffle* consisted of a simple block-and-tackle arrangement, lay on the coachroof, the boom-end having pulled free.

Bethany froze, one foot braced on a splintered remnant of the starboard-side bench seat and the other on the bottom edge of the companionway hatch.

Why couldn't she make herself go below?

Because she was afraid?

Surely not.

No, it was because of the overpowering silence.

No static from the radio, no crackle of burning joinery, no slosh of a flooding bilge.

No sound of any sort, only the stench left behind by the explosion ... and the nose-stinging bite of raw gasoline.

The varnish on the remaining woodwork around the companionway hatch sparkled in the sunlight.

Bethany went below.

~~*

Rajiv lay sprawled on the starboard settee, just as he would be if he'd been standing in front of the stove when it exploded.

But that wasn't right, either. Not exactly. It was wrong, take-it-to-the-bank wrong, but she couldn't think why. Her mind simply wouldn't lock.

Never mind.

Bethany rushed to him.

"Rajiv! Rajiv!"

She knelt down beside him. One of her knees ground into a scattering of broken glass, and she could feel it cut into her flesh.

She shook Rajiv, trying to snap him out of whatever fit he was having.

"What are you doing here?" she demanded. "You're supposed to be at home?"

She shook him again, but by now the hopelessness of it was apparent.

It was only then that her grief and her shock took hold. They left her feeling as numb as if she'd stayed in the water.

But what was he doing *here* of all places?

She'd left him behind in Coal Harbour, hadn't she? As she'd pulled away from their slip, he'd turned away and had walked back up the walk toward the parking garage, hadn't he?

She clearly remembered him doing exactly that.

Clearly.

But he evidently hadn't.

Rajiv's clothes were in ribbons. His eyes were open, staring fixedly up at the gap where the overhead had been. His lips were curled back from his teeth, making him look like a fresh-as-can-be version of one of those mummified Antarctic explorers who hadn't made it back alive. His life vest hadn't opened. There'd been no reason for it to. Black smudges covered his face. A lot of his hair, which had been thick and black, had burned away.

Rajiv had had the prettiest hair, the nicest smile, and Bethany had positively lost herself in his eyes, which were, or had been, the deepest, kindest, gentlest eyes she'd ever seen on a man.

Her stomach twisted, and as though she were emerging from a fit of her own, she remembered.

She had wanted to sail the boat across to Nanaimo to have some work done on it. Rajiv had wanted to have the work done in Vancouver, but she had argued for one of the yards in Nanaimo. She and Rajiv had fought, and she'd left the house without him.

She was perfectly capable of sailing across the Strait by herself. She'd done it countless times.

Like it or not, she wasn't about to bind either her hair or her feet or her life.

She had been warming up *Kerfuffle*'s engine when he'd come down the dock at Coal Harbour, dressed to go sailing.

"I've changed my mind," he had said, and hopped aboard.

Now, staring at his blast-contorted body, Bethany's eyes burned.

The boat rocked, and the sunlight slanted across the salon.

That was when Bethany noticed the rifle. It was lying on the cabin sole.

She recognized it immediately. It was Lizzy's hunting rifle, a lever-action .30-30, handed down from their paternal grandmother.

How had it gotten aboard?

How?

The memory wouldn't come.

Bethany was sure she hadn't brought it aboard. It was Lizzy's rifle, after all. What would Bethany have been doing with it?

Lizzy wouldn't have left it behind. She never borrowed the boat. Never came near the boat.

Another piece fell into place.

Lizzy hated the boat. She'd dutifully taken a look at it after Rajiv and Bethany had bought it, but that had been the one and only time Lizzy had ever been aboard.

No, that wasn't right, either.

Lizzy had—

Had what?

Bethany couldn't think.

Did she have a concussion?

Probably.

A mild one.

No double vision.

No loss of balance.

No screaming, pounding, blinding headache.

Just a garbled memory.

Rajiv, then, must have borrowed Lizzy's rifle and brought it aboard.

But why?

Bethany stared at the hunting weapon.

On a hunch, Bethany went forward to the forepeak, to the place where she and Rajiv slept, where they made love, when they were aboard overnight.

She stood there for a moment, trying to remember, afraid that she would. Hoping that she would not. Wasn't it enough that he was dead? Couldn't she be content with that?

No, she could not.

She compelled her recalcitrant, sluggish mind to focus, to focus, to focus, and then she remembered.

She snatched up the corner of the starboard cushion, the cushion that she slept on.

THE MUZZLE FLASH

Beneath it, she found a pair of tiger-striped panties. These, too, she recognized. She'd given them to Lizzy just last Christmas. Matching panties and bra, complete with an outrageous set of false fingernails. "A kitty's got to have claws." A sweep of her hooked fingers, slashing the air. "Grrr."

Bethany dropped the cushion back into place and returned aft.

She couldn't remember how she'd known that Lizzy and Rajiv were having an affair, but Bethany was certain that they had been. The panties proved as much.

How long had it been going on?

Months?

Years?

Days?

The boat rocked again. This time fairly heavily, and something rolled across the cabin sole. It rattled and flashed in the sunlight.

A brass cartridge casing.

Not the whole cartridge, just the spent brass. The neck was dirty with powder residue.

~~*

Bethany slumped on the port settee.

The explosion had thrown Rajiv across the salon. He'd wound up in the middle of the starboard settee, toward the forward end.

Her earlier disquiet returned in full force.

How had he ended up so far forward?

She tried to tell herself that it had happened because he hadn't been standing in front of the stove when the propane had exploded. If he had been, he would have ended up farther aft, much farther aft.

Or was her mind playing tricks on her. She was not, after all, any kind of a forensic scientist. Who could say how the explosion had behaved. It ought to have killed her, too, but instead it had thrown her clear.

No, that wouldn't wash. The only explanation was that he hadn't been standing in front of the stove when it had exploded. He hadn't been making coffee. He had been doing something else. All right. Fine. Perfect. Top marks, that shivering lady. But what had he been doing?

Another memory snapped into focus, bursting through her grief-fueled mental fog like an airliner crashing through the plate-glass windows of an airline terminal.

Bethany had inherited the family's Vancouver home, while Lizzy had received the vacation home and acreage on Cortes Island and the family boat, one of the Ed Monk power cruisers, now a genuine classic. The house in Vancouver, situated between Granville and the University of British Columbia, had never been a shack but it had never been a mansion, either. Nevertheless, thanks to a slew of factors, the house was now worth a small fortune.

Rajiv had worked up the numbers and had decided that selling the house would give him enough money to go into business for himself. Manufacturing cell-phone subassemblies and accessories. In India.

Why India?

Because India was the twenty-first century's land of opportunity.

It was an interesting scheme, about as interesting as a root canal, and about as practical as a two-wheeled lawnmower.

Rajiv was a middle-manager in one of his father's businesses, the automobile dealership. His degree was in business administration, not in engineering or manufacturing. He'd never so much as seen the inside of an electronics assembly plant, and he didn't speak Hindi.

"They speak English," he said. "Language won't be a problem."

Bethany and Rajiv had fought.

Of course.

Rajiv was desperate to get out from under his father's thumb.

Every time Bethany thought she'd settled the matter, Rajiv came back in a month or two with yet another scheme. They all began with selling the house and moving to India, or Johannesburg, or Singapore, or Australia, or Hong Kong. Argentina and then Mexico had been favorites for a time.

Bethany refused to budge.

"If you want to strike out on your own, fine. Go to Taiwan. But I'm staying here and I'm not selling the house. Maybe your family will bankroll you."

Eventually Rajiv had started crying on Lizzy's shoulder ... and doing other things to other parts of her anatomy.

And vice versa.

Good old Lizzy.

She never had gotten the hang of holding an aspirin between her knees.

It was time to leave the boat.

Right now.

Bethany couldn't say why, but the sooner she was gone, the better.

For one thing, the Coast Guard was bound to show up, and she wanted to be long gone before that happened.

But why?

Again that stupid question, repeating itself endlessly.

She didn't have any idea why, but she was dead certain she had to make it appear as though she'd been blown clear and that she hadn't been able to get back aboard.

A fire would do the trick.

If the boat had been burning, she couldn't have climbed back aboard, and without access to the radio, her only option would have been to paddle ashore.

Speaking of radios and communications, she fished out her smartphone and tossed it onto the shelf above the portside settee, next to the change jar, where it usually lived when they were out.

But without her smartphone, after she'd made it to shore, then what?

Duh! A payphone, naturally.

She grabbed a fistful of quarters, loonies, and toonies out of the change jar and stuffed them into a pocket.

Finally, she couldn't very well leave Lizzy's hunting rifle behind.

Why?

Again, no answer.

She felt like a ventriloquist's dummy, spouting lines and issuing pronouncements that someone else was feeding her.

But about the rifle ...

Maybe it wasn't any more complicated than the fact that it had belonged to their grandmother.

Certainties abounded.

Certainties were not explanations, but the certainties would have to do. At least for now. The details would come later. They had to.

Bethany scooped up the rifle and the spent brass. She unloaded the rifle and de-cocked it. The brass and the cartridges went into her pocket, and the rifle went into its carrying case, an olive-drab, softshell number that Lizzy said looked "too edgy for words." Then the rifle went into the kayak.

The leaking gasoline was sloshing under the Atomic 4.

Perfect.

Bethany built a likely pile of wood, paper, and fiberglass debris, positioning it at the bottom of the companionway ladder. She sprinkled a liberal dose of gasoline over it.

Then she lit one of Rajiv's cigarettes, American, of course, and used it and a book of paper matches to rig a fuse, just like in the movies.

Now came the tricky bit.

She wormed the fuse into the debris pile as far as she dared.

She was taking something of a stupid risk, but needs must. She wanted to make sure the damn thing worked.

Rajiv had brought the .30-30 with him.

"Lizzy asked me to run it down to that gunsmith in Sidney. Have him give it the once over."

It was then that Bethany had tumbled to the fact that things between Rajiv and Lizzy had progressed beyond the hanky-panky stage.

A trail of cigarette smoke rose from the pile of kindling, the time counting down, smoldering down.

Satisfied that she'd done what needed doing, Bethany went up into the cockpit, stopping to remove the blue masking tape from the propane sensor.

She didn't have the vaguest idea what the tape was doing there—a temporary repair of one sort or another—but she was certain that she had to remove it and take it with her.

She went aft, climbed down into her kayak, and shoved off.

She would have to dispose of the brass and the cartridges. Easy enough. She had a lot of water to pick from.

She paddled a few meters away from *Kerfuffle* and waited.

Rajiv had wanted to buy the boat, but Bethany had been the one who'd taken to sailing. Rajiv was more the hang-around-the-marina type. More the wannabe Royal Vancouver Yacht Club type. But he'd never had the moxie to pull it off. Being a young man on the make was all well and good, but being a young man *obviously and gauchely* on the make was something else again.

How a membership in the RVYC was supposed to have meshed with setting up a factory in Kuala Lumpur, he'd never explained.

"It's all part of the plan. You'll see. It'll be great. No worries."

A loud *Whump!* sounded from the boat and a column of black smoke rose from the companionway.

The town of Gibsons was almost due north, not that far away really. They had a marina and urgent care facilities. She had friends there, too. Janine. Bethany could trust Janine. Gibsons it was. Good choice.

Bethany began paddling.

The kayak slipped across the water. It knifed through the surface chop and rose and fell with the larger waves. The wind had died to a near calm.

As she worked, she began to warm up.

After a time, she looked back.

Flames were leaping from the hole left behind by the shattered coachroof, and above the flames rose an ugly stream of black smoke.

Even from as far away as she was, she could smell it, choking the very air.

As she was watching, a detonation ripped through the boat's stern. The gasoline fumes in the bilge had gone off, or maybe the gasoline tank had exploded. Whichever it had been, pieces of the cockpit combing and what was left of the benches flew into the air, much as she must have done.

It was too bad.

She'd always enjoyed *Kerfuffle*.

Right up to the point when she'd found her sister's panties in the V-berth.

How her sister had left them behind was anybody's guess. Maybe she'd done it deliberately. Maybe she'd suffered a spasm of carelessness. Whatever the case, it didn't matter. They'd been left behind, and even Lizzy couldn't have been stupid enough to have left them deliberately. Maybe Rajiv had kept them as a souvenir and had forgotten to take them along when he'd left the boat.

That was like Rajiv, the sort of thing he'd end up doing. Forgetful. Arrogant. Like selling cars and then not bothering to complete *all* of the required paperwork.

Several of the images drifting in her mental fog took on greater definition. It was like entering a marina at night. Only those images were welcome, whereas the ones Bethany was remembering were ugly, as ugly and as repellant as the flames devouring *Kerfuffle*.

Bethany hadn't bought the gunsmith malarkey for an instant. No, Rajiv had brought the rifle along to use on her.

His plan must have been simple. He'd been taking the gun over to Sidney, and he'd been giving it a onceover and there'd been a terrible accident. Poor Bethany. What a tragedy.

That would have been his story to the police, with Lizzy corroborating his every word through a flood of tears and hysterics. She was good at those, tears and hysterics.

That had only left the question of when. When would he make his move?

Out in the middle, of course, as far away from land and prying eyes and help as possible.

Bethany couldn't take the gun away from him. She could try, but if she failed, he'd kill her with it on the spot. Bullet for one, no waiting.

Which had left Bethany at a loss ... until she thought of the stove and the nature of propane.

As they were nearing the middle of the Strait, she volunteered to make coffee.

Playing the loving and dutiful husband, he took the tiller.

"We really ought to install wheel steering," he said.

"Good idea. I'll talk to the yard about it," she said, and went below.

She thought that now she had a chance to find the rifle and throw it overboard, but that wouldn't solve the bigger problem. True, it would dispose of Rajiv's "weapon of choice," but a boat was nothing if not a storehouse of potential weapons. No, dumping the rifle overboard wouldn't solve a thing.

THE MUZZLE FLASH

Sticking to her own plan, she went to work in the galley.

She deliberately dropped the teakettle.

It made a metallic bang followed by a lot of rattling.

"Sorry," she called.

"Everything okay?" Rajiv answered, Mr. Concern and Consideration.

"Butter fingers. No worries."

She clattered around for a while longer, making a show of it, but in the process she managed to wrap the propane sensor—the leak-detecting end of the alarm system—with blue masking tape. What it couldn't detect it couldn't report.

The kettle whistled and she turned it off.

She made two cups of coffee.

Rajiv took his with sugar. She drank hers black.

She put honey in his. He liked honey, and he'd appreciate the thought. Thoughtful Bethany. Normal as normal, eh?

She turned the burner back on but did not light it.

The escaping gas made a faint hiss.

Being heavier than air, the propane would collect in the bilges and build up over the cabin sole. Anyone standing in the cabin, however, wouldn't necessarily smell it, not immediately. That's why the sensors were always mounted down as low as possible.

Unlike Rajiv, Bethany *had* studied engineering, and was doing rather nicely at it, too.

Bethany took the tiller. They drank their coffee and chatted about life in Vancouver, about the yard that would be working on the boat, and about Rajiv's latest hopes for getting into the RVYC.

He finished his coffee and rather than setting the empty cup aside in a corner, he took it below.

THE GREAT MYSTERY OF ETERNITY

~~*

Here it came.

Now or never.

Thank you, Lizzy.

Thank you, Rajiv.

Rot in hell, the pair of you.

"What's that smell?" he called up.

"Nothing," she answered. "I had a little trouble lighting the stove."

"Oh. It's awfully strong."

"I had a lot of trouble," she said. "It'll air out."

"Let's hope."

It was everything she could do not to flinch, not to give the game away by running.

She heard him moving around, positioning himself. He was on the port side, far enough forward to give himself an unobstructed shot up through the companionway.

Silence.

She was certain that if she looked down through the open hatch she'd see him aiming the rifle at her, see the black maw of the .30-30's muzzle gazing back at her.

The boat was pitching and rolling.

Under these circumstances, a rifle shot, even at close range, stood a damn good chance of missing. Rajiv had to be shaking, frightened out of his wits. He'd be doing good to aim the rifle and pull the trigger, let along *squeeze* it.

He was bound to miss.

He was a miserable shot. Even when he took his—

The muzzle flash lit up the boat's interior.

THE MUZZLE FLASH

Then came the explosion.
And then came the report.
All within microseconds.
And Bethany was hurtling through the air, just like a mortar shell.
Too much propane.

~~*

By the time Bethany had the Parsley Islands off to her starboard and Gibsons off her port bow, the early evening gloom had begun to harden into night, and the temperature had dropped.

Well, it would, wouldn't it? It being night and all.

Which by a series of connections reminded her of a task left unfinished.

She wormed the cartridges and the spent casing out of her pocket and dropped them overboard.

Good-bye, good-bye. Rest in peace.

Just how many shots had Rajiv intended to use on her?

Never mind. He'd probably stuffed cartridges into the magazine until it wouldn't take any more.

The dunce.

As for the hunting rifle itself, Bethany planned to return it to Lizzy, its rightful owner, her own dear, loving, slut of a sister.

What a joyous reunion it would be.

Bethany's arms ached and she was chilled to the bone. Her teeth were chattering and she was shivering from the top of her head to the bottoms of her feet. No, the survival blanket from the first-aid kit hadn't helped much. Nor had the paddling.

THE GREAT MYSTERY OF ETERNITY

~~*

It was pitch black by the time Bethany made it through the rocky channel between Keats Island and Gibsons.

She entered the marina, spotted an empty slip, and paddled into it.

The finger walk was a very nice finger walk, just the sort of thing she'd been looking for, but in her current state of shock and exhaustion and hypothermia, she couldn't even begin to climb out of her kayak and up onto it. It was too bloody high.

She paddled out of the slip.

She eventually found the dinghy dock, which was low to the water and not terribly well lit.

Good.

It was too soon for harsh light.

The night cossetted her.

She tied up her kayak and managed to flop, harbour-seal fashion, onto the dock.

She lay there, on her back, looking up, seeing and not seeing at the same time.

After a time, she levered herself onto her feet. When the rush of dizziness had subsided she went in search of a payphone.

After looking in the breezeway near the marina's office, she went around the building and found a phone near the marina's laundromat.

And it was in working order.

She fed the coin slot and punched in the number.

Click.

Click.

Ringing.

THE MUZZLE FLASH

Janine, the friend who lived in Gibsons, answered.

Bethany came right to the point. "I'm in Gibsons. Down at the marina. Could you be a dear and come pick me up?"

Consternation on the other end, then, "Of course I'll pick you up, but what's happened?"

Bethany collapsed back onto the wall next to the telephone. She gazed up at the night-black clouds. "I'm afraid there's been a rather nasty kerfuffle aboard *Kerfuffle*," she said.

FR. ANDREI MEETS COMRADE STALIN

Quite unexpectedly, an Orthodox priest meets the ghost of Comrade Stalin. The ghost is sitting quietly in the nave of the priest's church. Why is he there? What does he want? And what is St. Seraphim of Sarov's role in all of this?

FR. ANDREI ILYICH ORLOV, archpriest and pastor of St. Seraphim of Sarov Orthodox Church in Edmonds, Washington, unlocked the front door to the church proper and went inside, gratefully.

Built in the 1970s on a budget that had been anything but lavish, the church was on the smallish side, but it had clean, reassuring lines, and its proportions were perfect for the parish, given its modest membership.

The nave was excitingly overcrowded at Pascha, people pressed together in the joy of the Resurrection, Sundays were cramped but manageable, and, usually, the Saturday vespers services were wonderfully comfortable, with plenty of room for people to spread out, for family groups to stand together without crowding.

Fr. Andrei closed and relocked the door.

Outside, the weather was truly grim, sullen to the point of being foul. It was the middle of winter, late in the day, and precious little light filtered in through the windows. Thus the interior of the church, with the lights off and none of the lampadas lit, was quite dim, nearly dark, darker than one would expect given the size of the windows.

The air was heavy with the aroma of the incense and the candles burned hours, days ago. The icons on the iconostasis looked down into the nave, their expressions a combination of love, judgment, and mercy. The ultimate challenge. Feed my sheep.

If there is no love, how can there be judgment, and if there is no judgment, how can there be mercy, and if there is no mercy, how can there be love, and if there is no love, how can anything be alive? For that matter, how can anything exist?

Elementary theology, but a pivotal riddle, nonetheless.

One of countless others.

How he missed them! Their challenge. Their fascination. Their company.

Inexpensive oriental carpets covered the floor of the nave, and a chandelier hung above it. There were no pews and no benches, but chairs stood in ranks across the back and up along the sides.

Their delightful intractability.

Icons covered the walls and the support posts. They were in rough groupings: American saints here, Russian saints there, Church hierarchs in another place. The groups, however, were so rough and so arbitrary that the arrangement amounted to nothing but a jumble, like the family photographs on a fireplace mantle.

Come to that, how Fr. Andrei missed the Church!

He walked on into the nave. He loved to be alone in the church, to drink in that special silence that only a place of worship can provide.

His missing the Church: the emotion was absurd on the face of it. He was a baptized and chrismated Orthodox Christian, after all. He was a priest, the pastor of a congregation. He was *in* the Church.

FR. ANDREI MEETS COMRADE STALIN

But there it was, that sense of grief. Yes, call it that.

Perhaps he ought to have followed the academic route. Perhaps he ought to have stuck it out and earned his doctorate. He could have taught and written. It would have been a good life, a productive one.

It had been suggested, but he had chosen the parish life.

He could un-choose it. He was still young enough to go back to school.

Yes, but would the result of that really be any better?

Probably not.

His sense of separation would undoubtedly linger, holding him captive.

He supposed that at one time or another, everyone felt *outside*, felt as though *meaning*, as though *authentic faith*, as though *the Church* were *over there*, not over *here*.

On an impulse, Fr. Andrei looked back toward the narthex. It was only then that he saw him.

Again.

He was seventy-four years old and was sitting in one of the chairs at the very back of the nave. He was stocky, and dressed in the Communist Party uniform typical of the '20s, '30s, and '40s. His face was pockmarked, but his mustache was thick. His hair was combed straight back from his forehead. His eyes were closed.

If the man's eyes had not been closed, Fr. Andrei knew he would be looking into perhaps the cruelest eyes that God had ever seen fit to set in a man's head.

Fr. Andrei's stomach clenched, not in fear, but in revulsion.

Without speaking, he looked away and left the church through a side door, passing by on the other side.

Behind him, automatically, the door swept closed, and the latch clicked home.

The church was safely locked.

Fr. Andrei crossed the narrow courtyard to the parish hall. He unlocked the building and went inside.

In his office, he hung his hat and coat on an antique coat tree, the sort of thing that would have been popular in the '20s, a donation from the estate of one of the parish's founding members. May her memory be eternal!

He switched on the lights, and tried to forget the man in the church.

Fr. Andrei sighed.

The lights had only worsened his mood. They amplified the papers scattered across his desk, the piles of books—some read, others waiting to be read—and the disordered stack of the church's unanswered mail on the credenza.

The credenza was a blond-veneer, Danish-modern piece from the '80s. It was another donation, and had come from the estate of a longtime parish elder. May his memory be eternal!

This afternoon, the icons in the icon corner of Fr. Andrei's office seemed to be taking him to task for his slovenly work habits.

The last several weeks had been hectic, and he'd allowed things to slip. Badly. He had no excuse and no wish to make one. Hectic was merely a fact, pure and simple. Well, it was more of a statement of opinion. An evasion, perhaps? Whatever the objective case, he promised to do better. He had to do better; if he didn't, he soon wouldn't be able to find anything, let alone accomplish anything worth accomplishing.

Fine.

What the lights did not amplify was the old man. Not the one

FR. ANDREI MEETS COMRADE STALIN

sitting in the church, but another one. An old man of an entirely different sort: a monk, a staretz. Apart from his icon, he was nowhere to be seen ... in Fr. Andrei's office.

Which, at the moment, was a good thing.

He could have followed across from the church, but he hadn't.

No small mercy, that.

Oh, well.

It was time to get down to it.

No doubt on that score.

Time and past.

But first a pot of tea.

Unaccountably ill-at-ease, Fr. Andrei left his office and crossed the parish hall to the kitchen.

There, he brewed himself a pot of tea. He despised tea. Yes, yes, he was a good Russian. In point of fact, he was of good Imperial Russian stock, via Alaska, via San Francisco, via China. And because he was, the absolute love of tea ought to have been implanted in his genes, but he secretly despised the stuff. He adored coffee to the point of idolatry, but now was not the time for coffee. It was the time for tea.

The worst part of the whole mess was that he made wretched tea. If he could make halfway decent tea, if he had had that blessing, his situation vis-à-vis tea wouldn't have been so bad, but the tea he made tasted like the tannin-choked spring runoff from a rainforest in British Columbia. There were even times when he could swear that he could taste the granite, too.

His wife, Yelena, on the other hand, made excellent tea. He almost enjoyed her tea. Eagerly. Truly.

She'd shown him how to make tea dozens, if not hundreds, of times, and he always made it exactly the way she'd shown him, but the tea he made invariably turned out to be insipid or acidic or both.

This time it had turned out to be acidic. He could tell by the exsanguinated aroma that was rising from the pot.

He sighed.

Acidic would have to do.

He draped a cozy over the pot and carried it and two cups and two saucers back to his office.

He poured a cup for himself, stirred in a packet of sugar, and waited.

It didn't take long.

The humble knock sounded on his door almost immediately.

Fr. Andrei recognized that knock, its cadence and its tone. With a glance at the icon of St. Seraphim of Sarov that hung in his icon corner, Fr. Andrei called, "Come on in, Batushka. Yes, yes, I've made tea."

Without bothering to open the door, a stooped old man entered Fr. Andrei's office. To say that he was stooped was to understate his situation. An injury to his back had left him permanently bent at the waist, as though he had been frozen in the midst of bowing. He had a round face and was wearing a monk's robe, tied with a length of rope. A finger-worn chotki hung from the rope. The man had long white hair and a full white beard. His face glowed, glowed to the point of shimmering.

His eyes were bottomless, impossible to look into for long without the risk of going mad, or of discovering the truth of one's own existence, which was very close to being the same thing.

He was St. Seraphim of Sarov, the patron saint of the parish Fr. Andrei pastored.

FR. ANDREI MEETS COMRADE STALIN

"The tea?" St. Seraphim asked. "Did your lovely wife make it?"

Fr. Andrei shrugged. "No, Sema. You know perfectly well that I made it myself. Why do you play such silly games?"

"I was being polite, my joy. Making conversation." He smiled mischievously. "Often I don't pay as much attention as I ought to. You see, at my age, my mind tends to wander."

"Your mind has *never* wandered, Batushka."

Batushka ... The word meant little father. It was a nickname, a diminutive, an expression of deep respect, of love. It was thoroughly appropriate for this Russian and North American favorite.

Fr. Andrei gestured with the pot. "Yes or no?"

"Your wife makes delicious tea."

"I know. On the other hand, mine stinks."

"You ought to have her teach you."

"You know I have, Batushka. Repeatedly."

"Try again. I'm sure you've almost got it."

Fr. Andrei scoffed. "Yes or no?"

"Yes, I'd love some," St. Seraphim said. "Hot tea is good for my old bones."

"You don't have bones."

"I do so."

"Not here, you don't."

"Not true. There's a fragment of me in the reliquary over in the church."

"It's a piece of one of your cassocks. Or so I'm told."

Sema looked slightly offended. "It's impolite to quibble."

Fr. Andrei poured. "Sugar?"

"Do bees make honey?"

Fr. Andrei mixed in three packets of sugar and handed Sema

the cup on a matching saucer. They had a floral pattern, large red flowers and lots of greenery.

Sema accepted his tea, with a happy smile. "Your wife's tea tastes better, Andrusha, but yours is stronger." He took a long drink. "I like strong tea. Strong, sweet tea is a cure for virtually anything."

Just how a non-corporeal being, a saint of the Orthodox Church, could hold a cup and saucer and drink tea was one of the questions Fr. Andrei was always meaning to explore but never did. He told himself that the resurrected Christ had eaten a piece of fish in the presence of the apostles and that he had also broken bread with two of the disciples on the road to Emmaus.

Sadly, that wasn't the same thing at all, however. The resurrected Christ was a flesh-and-blood person, whereas St. Seraphim was, for the time being at least, pure spirit.

In any event, at the moment, this non-answer was as much of an answer as he needed, as much of an answer as he wanted.

Sema set his cup on the edge of a handy bookcase.

"You'd hoped that I'd drop by," Sema said. "That's the reason for the tea, isn't it? A bribe."

"Yes."

"I thought as much."

"That fellow sitting in the church, do you have any idea what he's doing *here*?"

"He has to be somewhere."

"Come on, Batushka. Seriously."

Sema cocked his head to one side. "Do you have any idea who he is?"

"How could I not know who he is?"

"Well, then? Who is he?"

FR. ANDREI MEETS COMRADE STALIN

"He's Comrade Stalin."

"No, actually, he was born Ioseb Besarionis Dze Jugashvili, in the town of Gori in Georgia, which at that time was a part of the Russian Empire. Iosif Vissarionovich Dzhugashvili is his name's Russian form. The date of his birth, as far as anyone can reliably tell, was December 18, 1878. It was only later, much later, that he became the dread Comrade Stalin, tyrant and mass murderer." St. Seraphim smiled, as he always did before telling an outrageous joke. "Iosif the Terrible, you might say."

"Thanks for the lecture."

"I do my best, my joy."

Fr. Andrei arched an eyebrow. "*Later*? You said *later*. Are you working up to telling me that we ought to excuse his unspeakable crimes because he endured a horrific childhood?"

"I most certainly am not. God forbid. Nevertheless, it is important to bear in mind such matters. Besides, in the ultimate sense, it isn't up to either of us either to condemn or to forgive him."

A little grudgingly, Fr. Andrei said, "That true."

Sema sipped his tea. "I suggest you ask him."

"Ask him what?"

"Ask him what he's doing here, of course."

"I'd rather carry a scorpion across a river."

Sema chuckled, and returned his empty cup to Fr. Andrei. "It's up to you," he said. "The tea was delicious. Just the thing on a cold afternoon. Thank you. Yes, I'd love another cup, but, no, thank you, it's time I was on my way. Say hello to Yelena for me."

And then his was gone.

He didn't exactly vanish, but he didn't exactly walk out

through the door, either. The whole comings-and-goings thing had taken Fr. Andrei a lot of time to get used to. It still caused a cold sweat to break out in the small of his back.

Where did the tea *go*? What happened to it?

And Fr. Andrei's original question remained unanswered. What was Stalin doing here of all places? What did he want?

Ask him.

Well, maybe it was time.

After all, Comrade Stalin had been hanging around the church for several days, now. When the weather was fine, he sat on one of the benches outside. When it was rainy or heavily overcast or at night, he sat inside, always in the nave. Often he stood. Usually, he kept his eyes closed, but sometimes he kept them open, and when they were he seemed to be looking at the icons on the iconostasis.

As far as Fr. Andrei could tell, for the most part, Stalin gazed at the icon on the Theotokos.

Was he thinking about his mother, that poor woman?

The contemplation of the Mother of God often led to a deeper consideration of one's own mother, one's own family. Was that what was going on? Was he thinking about his son? About his daughter?

Ask him.

Was Stalin begging the Theotokos to intercede for him with her son?

If that were true, there would be no end of a hideous irony in it. When Stalin had had the chance, he had refused to intercede on behalf of his eldest son, Yakov.

However ...

The son of the Theotokos was right there, on the opposite side

FR. ANDREI MEETS COMRADE STALIN

of the Royal Doors. If Stalin wanted to, he could appeal directly to Him.

If Stalin, the onetime seminarian, could bring himself to take that step ...

What was Comrade Stalin doing?

Ask him.

The words echoed back and forth through Fr. Andrei's mind. They repeated themselves in Sema's voice—gentle, determined, a suggestion rather than a dictate, an invitation rather than a command.

"Phooey," Fr. Andrei said aloud.

He slipped on his jacket, locked his office, and went back into the church proper.

Comrade Stalin had changed places. He was still in the back row, but now he was on the left side, on the aisle.

Fr. Andrei sat down opposite him, on the right side, also on the aisle. It felt like the safest place to be, with the aisle between them.

Fr. Andrei waited, and while he waited, he thought about what Sema had said to him. He thought about the horrors that the man across the aisle from him had committed, that he had ordered others to commit, that others had been only too eager to commit for him, and that still others had committed in reaction.

Fr. Andrei also thought about human judgment, and about the knowledge of good and evil, and about the Fall.

He thought about the Last Judgment, the Dread Day.

Dread, indeed.

For how, considering the limited nature of human nature, was anyone to tell the difference between good and evil?

Comrade Stalin asked, "What are you doing here?"

The breath caught in Fr. Andrei's throat.

He looked across.

Stalin's eyes were open, and just as Fr. Andrei had imagined, they were filled with an implacable cruelty. Were they Stalin's father's eyes? Or were they the eyes, sly and pitiless, that his life had earned him?

"I'm the pastor of this church," Fr. Andrei said.

"Ah, so you're the one who cheats the babas out of their last miserable kopeks."

Comrade Stalin hadn't smiled, had done nothing to give the game away, but it was plain that he was teasing, rather than taunting, Fr. Andrei. Stalin was nothing if not the master of the cutting jest.

Fr. Andrei had been primed to take offense at anything the old dictator might say or do, but in the event, now that it had arrived, Fr. Andrei found that he wasn't the least bit offended. Stalin, it seemed, alive or dead, had a certain inexplicable and dumbfounding aura about him.

Uncle Joe, indeed.

Fr. Andrei said, "No, like as not, I'm the one who stops them from stealing the candle money. They're welcome to as many candles as they want, but not to the money."

"Spoken like a true exploiter of the toiling masses."

Fr. Andrei bowed slightly, acknowledging the sarcastic compliment. "The workers, peasants, and working intellectuals would be proud of you for pointing that out."

"The ones who are still alive," Stalin said. "There are so few of us left in these pathetic, bourgeois days." Stalin's expression lost its spark.

"Why are you here?" Fr. Andrei asked.

FR. ANDREI MEETS COMRADE STALIN

"Death has a way of changing one's perspective," Comrade Stalin said. "Imagine my surprise when I realized that my death had *not* resulted in my annihilation? It started me thinking."

"About what?"

"Does God exist? Do those millions of dead exist? My victims? The people I executed for crimes against the state?"

"And?"

Stalin sighed. "I don't know about God, but they *do* exist."

"It makes a certain amount of sense. If you exist, then they ought to exist, too."

"They do," Stalin said, with a finality that left no room for doubt. "Absolutely. Inescapably."

Reflexively, Fr. Andrei looked, and to his shock and horror, he saw that people thronged the nave. They were Stalin's victims: the starved, shot, frozen, poisoned, beaten, stabbed, diseased, cannibalized. The suicides. The desperate, the betrayed, the guilty, the innocent. The cynics and the idealists and the ones who simply hadn't given a damn. Men, women, and children. The young and the old. In their tens of millions.

Each of them was gazing hungrily at Comrade Stalin.

Fr. Andrei asked, "Why are they here?"

Comrade Stalin arched an eyebrow. "You really are a very stupid fellow, aren't you? They're here to tear me apart."

A wave of realization passed through Fr. Andrei. "Only they can't because we're on holy ground."

"Exactly," Comrade Stalin said.

Sanctuary ...

Comrade Stalin gestured contemptuously at his victims. "They refuse to move on."

Yes, that much was clear. They had, rather self-evidently,

chosen revenge over everything and everyone else. "Perhaps if you were to move on, they would, too."

"Are you offering to hear my confession?"

"Do you want to confess?"

"I have nothing to confess," Comrade Stalin said. "But, no, I will never move *on*." He shrugged, smiled. "I move *around*. Lenin's tomb, then that place by the Kremlin wall. Who knows where they'll put me next?"

"It's an uncertain world," Fr. Andrei said.

"Indeed it is."

The church's heating-and-cooling system switched on. The fans made a low susurration, and Fr. Andrei could feel the movement of the air, smell the paradoxically heightened aroma of the incense and the candles, burned hours ago.

"You ought to light the lampadas," Comrade Stalin said. "All this gloom. It's bad for the psyche."

"In what way?"

"It leaves people wondering what's lurking in the shadows."

"I find it restful."

"You would."

Fr. Andrei chose to answer the challenge with one of his own. "Why is that?"

Comrade Stalin resettled himself in his chair. "So tell me, Andrei Ilyich, what about you? When will you move on?"

"Move on? Move on from what?"

"Ah, priest, I know you better than you think I do."

"What are you talking about?"

"When will the scales fall from your eyes? When will you see through the sham of your own greed?"

Fr. Andrei's surprise was genuine. "What greed?"

FR. ANDREI MEETS COMRADE STALIN

"Your hunger for piety, your lust of certainty?"

"I'm not greedy!"

Comrade Stalin arched an eyebrow. "When will you come to your senses and settle for mere *faith*?" He smirked, an inquisitor leagues ahead of his suspect. "When, Andrei Ilyich, will *you* move on? When will your ears stop itching?"

But to this question Fr. Andrei could frame no satisfactory answer.

THE BANK TELLER

This historical sea-faring tale takes place ashore. The place is Port Townsend, Washington, back around the turn of the 20th century. In those days, when the sail-powered international lumber trade was at its height, Port Townsend was a wild-and-wooly center for shanghaiing.

A lot of sailors accepted the practice as just another one of the hazards of their trade. But not all of them did ...

HE STOPPED AT THE TOP of the hill above Port Townsend and set his suitcase down on the pavement. He stretched his back, worked his injured leg, and scanned back along the way he had come. Only three other people were on the street, and he had seen none of them down by the harbor. No one had followed him up the hill.

It was a bright summer afternoon, and the air away from downtown smelled of trees and flowers, rather than horse dung and cooking grease. Off to the southeast, out in Port Townsend Bay, two full-rigged ships, a steamer, and three lumber schooners rode at anchor. A tug was heading to the southwest.

It amused him to think how readily he had identified the rigs. How quickly he had learned the seaman's trade. He'd actually enjoyed that part of it, the learning and the work itself.

Farther out, to the east and northeast, lay Admiralty Inlet, the northernmost end of Puget Sound, lumberyard to the world. He felt an odd sense of pride in that and a much odder sense of having come home.

After five years.

When he'd left, it had been the 19th century, and now it was the 20th. A line crossed. The equator, too. He'd become a shellback.

With yet another line waiting for him to cross.

But all in good time.

He turned his back on the water, on the way he had come. He picked up his suitcase and walked on.

He'd bought his suitcase used at a pawnshop in Portland, Oregon, but he'd bought his shoes new in Seattle. They were good shoes, heavy and durable, and he could smell the new smell rising off of them. But they were too new to be comfortable. His feet hurt, and because of it, his injured leg was acting up and his limp was becoming more noticeable with every step.

The limp was neither here nor there, but he had no wish to become memorable, no wish to be identifiable as a man with a limp.

He wondered how much farther he would have to go before he reached the New Bedford House.

Ten minutes later he was standing in front of the New Bedford, identified as such by a small sign hanging above the steps leading up to the front porch. The building was a large, three-story house with a mansard roof. The siding was white, and the trim was gray. There was a fussy yard, complete with flower beds and a kitchen garden.

He climbed the steps. An engraved brass plaque next to the front door announced the New Bedford to be a gentlemen's boarding house. He rang the bell.

THE BANK TELLER

~~*

The door was opened by Mrs. Cornelia Abbott, the owner. She was a stout woman in her middle fifties. Her her eyes were keen and quick and pale blue.

They sat in the parlor, which was at the front of the house. He was glad to be off his feet, to give his leg a chance to rest.

The furniture was old but in good condition. The cloth upholstery was worn but not threadbare. The room was clean and in good order. An oil portrait of a sea captain hung over the fireplace. A brass plate identified the subject as Captain Ezekiel Makepeace Abbott, 1847—1893.

A slip of a girl brought tea and disappeared wordlessly back into the recesses of the house.

The tea was strong, and the conversation dispensed with the business at hand in short order. He wanted a room; she had one to let. He wanted quiet; she insisted on it. He never drank to excess; she evicted drunks without hesitation.

She ran the most respectable boarding house in Port Townsend; he insisted on nothing less. It was comparatively expensive; he could afford it.

She took him into her office. It was a compact, overcrowded room that had probably once been the sea captain's study. It smelled of paper and furniture polish. She sat him at a table and put the register in front of him. She provided pen and ink.

"Please sign the book," she said.

"It would be my pleasure," he said, and picked up the pen.

He studied the empty, waiting line.

What name should he give her?

Not his own, surely, although that was likely to be safe

enough. *Likely* ...

In the end, he gave her the name they had given him five years ago: Johan Schmidt. He'd gone by Smitty, mostly. Sometimes John. Sometimes Jack. The names had followed around the world. They had carried him from one life into another. It was only fitting that they should carry him back.

But he wasn't that stupid.

Five years couldn't be stripped away, erased as though they had never happened.

That said, however, it might be possible to achieve some measure of balance. Barely. Now that he had returned to Port Townsend.

He signed his name as *Johan Schmidt*. He added his arrival date: July 15, 1901.

She read the line and seemed quite satisfied. "An educated hand, Mr. Schmidt," she said, and gave him a slight nod. "Welcome to the New Bedford."

"Thank you for allowing me to stay," Schmidt said, and counted out his rent.

Mrs. Abbott said, "Breakfast is at six thirty, and supper at six o'clock. We ring a gong fifteen minutes ahead. Late arrivals may eat in the kitchen."

She handed him a receipt, a key to the front door, and a key to his room.

~~*

Schmidt's room was at the front and provided a good view of the street and the bay and a snowcapped mountain off in the distance to the east, but not of the Strait of Juan de Fuca.

THE BANK TELLER

The room was large. It had a bed, a wardrobe, a washstand with a blue-and-white enameled pitcher and basin, a shaving mirror on the wall above the washstand, a table and chair, a nightstand next to the bed, a kerosene lamp, a box of matches, and a red-and-blue rug. A coat hook had been fastened to the wall next to the door.

He unpacked his suitcase and took off his shoes. He locked the door and hung his jacket and hat on the hook.

With those tasks out of the way, he lay down on the bed. It was neither too hard nor too soft, neither too large nor too small. It was just right. He felt like Goldilocks.

He did, however, choose to leave his revolver, a short-barreled Colt, secured in its shoulder holster, readily available.

He closed his eyes and allowed his mind to wander.

He'd bought his gun, his shoes, and his suit in Seattle before coming over on a steamer. He liked Seattle, what he'd seen of it. He imagined that someday he might settle there.

In the meantime, he had work to do. Apropos of which, he wondered what sort of people his fellow lodgers were.

The gong woke Schmidt out of a sound sleep.

He pulled on his suit coat and went down to dinner.

The dining-room table was piled with food, while around it were crowded five men and Mrs. Abbott, who sat—Where else?—at the head of the table. She had a small brass bell within easy reach. She'd changed into a more elaborate dress and tidied her hair.

There was an empty chair at the foot, not directly opposite

her, which would have never done, but to her right. She waved him toward it.

Mrs. Abbott introduced him and offered only that he was newly arrived in town. The names of the five men as well as the men themselves blurred into a haze that was neither effusive nor aloof.

Schmidt hoped he would be able to remember the names when called upon.

Mrs. Abbott led her guests in saying grace, which they did with their heads respectfully, if not reverently, bowed. At the *Amen* the man across the table from Schmidt crossed himself in the Roman Catholic manner, left shoulder then right, rather than in the Orthodox Christian manner, right shoulder then left.

At Mrs. Abbott's instruction, the plates of food began to make the rounds.

~~*

After dinner, Schmidt went out onto the front porch. The weather had remained fine, and the evening air was balmy but held the first chill of the approaching night. It reminded him of San Francisco.

A man walked over and stood next to him, the one who'd crossed himself. He was thin and neatly dressed to the point of being prim. He had ink stains on the fingers of his right hand.

"Evening," the man said.

"Evening," Schmidt said, and scrambled for the man's name. Charles McNeill. No, that wasn't it. *Clayton* McNeill. Yes, that was it. Clayton. "Beautiful evening, isn't it, Mr. McNeill?"

"Yes, it is," McNeill said. He looked from side to side, then

THE BANK TELLER

asked, "I don't mean to pry, but what's your line of work?"

"Bookkeeper," Schmidt said, and told himself to roll with the conversation. He'd known there would be questions, and here they were.

"You have the look of a sailor."

Schmidt smiled as warmly as he could—jovial, friendly, unthreatening. "I was a sailor."

"Recently?"

Schmidt laughed, a little self-consciously. "Until a few days ago, yes."

"Ship's purser, I'd say."

"Correct again." Schmidt smiled as though he were enjoying the conversation immensely. He wasn't. "You're very astute."

"No, not really. What with your limp and all, it pretty much had to be purser, cook, or sailmaker. But your hands aren't beat up enough for you to have been a sailmaker, and you don't have the look of a cook. So that left purser."

There was, evidently, no possibility of hiding the limp. Schmidt said, "Process of elimination, then?"

"Something like that. Were you always a purser?"

"No, only after I acquired the limp."

"How was that? If you don't mind my asking."

"I fell down a companionway ladder."

"You were lucky," McNeill said.

"So I've been told," Schmidt answered. It was hard for him to keep his voice relaxed, but five years at sea, and several bucko mates, had taught him that, too.

"You any good? With numbers, I mean."

"Good enough to make a living at it."

"Looking for work?"

"Depends," Schmidt said.

McNeill handed him a business card. It identified him as a bookkeeper with the Olympic Lumbermens Bank of Commerce. "Come by tomorrow morning. Eleven o'clock or thereabouts. The bank's looking for a teller."

"Thanks," Schmidt said, and pocketed the card. It was more, much more, than he could have hoped for.

"Don't forget," McNeill said. "Eleven." He nodded and walked out to the street. He turned and walked off to the southwest.

Schmidt followed but turned in the opposite direction, to the northeast, toward Morgan Hill, toward the corner of Grant and Madison.

The house that occupied the north corner of Grant and Madison was a mansion by Port Townsend standards. It had three floors, dozens of windows, trim so ornate that it made the New Bedford look like the country cousin, and an observation turret. The house was everything that local fashion demanded. And it was ablaze with light. It shouted wealth and influence and power.

It was the home of Captain Douglas Victor Hansen, sea captain and ship owner, and it made the man who went by the name of Johan Schmidt feel small and powerless and easily crushed.

The next morning at eleven o'clock, Schmidt presented himself to Clayton McNeill at the Olympic Lumbermens bank. McNeill handed him over to George Lindauer, the head teller, and

THE BANK TELLER

by two o'clock that afternoon, Schmidt had the job.

He had nothing to do now but work at his new job and watch and wait.

~~*

Olympic Lumbermens was down on the flat, on the inboard side of Water Street. It was not far from several of the town's landmarks: the Union Wharf, the Paris Opera House, the infamous Blue Star Saloon, and the notorious Gloucester Arms Residential Hotel. The bank was directly across from the worst Shanghaiing den of the lot: the Mariner's Rest, which was owned by none other than Captain Douglas Victor Hansen.

However, regardless of which place a footloose man picked, he stood a good chance of paying for his lodging or his meal or his entertainment with a fit of sudden unconsciousness and a voyage to the Orient.

And sooner or later, everyone, from the owners to the stable boys, came through the bank. Schmidt remembered their names and where they worked, and he never failed to smile and ask how they were doing. Everyone agreed that the bank's new teller was a real gentleman. It was just plain too bad about his limp, though, the poor man.

The poor man made notes.

He read the shipping columns, the society columns, the business pages, and the shipping registers. He read current issues and he read back issues. Page by page, he gleaned that the resident of the house at Grant and Madison was active in his church, was shrewdly expanding his business holdings, was a major contributor to the Port Townsend Policeman's Trust, and was also a major contributor to the current mayor's political campaigns and favored causes.

The jewel in the crown, however, was the information that two years ago, he had retired from his career afloat in order to devote his full energies to the betterment of his community.

Schmidt recorded the comings and goings, the schedules. He wrote down arrival and departure times, especially those of Captain Hansen, but also those of two particular runners: Jimmy "Shanghai Rooster" Gibson and Harry "No Ears" Pederson.

Jimmy "Shanghai Rooster" Gibson worked as a bartender for Big Mike Gamble, who owned the Blue Star Saloon. Big Mike was Port Townsend's so-called King of the Crimps. Like Hansen, he, too, was a stalwart contributor to the Port Townsend Policeman's Trust. As it turned out, Big Mike was Hansen's only serious competition.

Harry "No Ears" Pederson occupied a rung much farther down the social ladder from the one occupied by Jimmy "Shanghai Rooster" Gibson. Nevertheless, No Ears fell within Big Mike's orbit. He filled in at the Blue Star's bar, swept the place out, and did "odd jobs."

The days went by, the pages of Schmidt's notebook filled up, and the picture grew from a vague sketch to a roughed-in landscape.

On September 5, 1901, the arrival of the four-masted bark *Susan B. Shattuck* ended Schmidt's wait.

~~*

The *Susan B. Shattuck* was a hellship, always had been. Five years ago Douglas Victor Hansen had been her proud owner and courageous captain. But he'd seen the handwriting on the wall—the irreversible advent of steam—and had sold out to his chief mate. Hansen's chief mate, then her new captain, had soon gone bankrupt and had sold her to her current pair or owners: Captain Lars "Blockhead" Burgess and his chief mate, Bully Johnson.

And through all the changes, nothing about her had changed, except that she had grown older and more tattered. She never sailed with a full crew, she fed her hands starvation rations, and she made do with worn-out equipment. Occasionally, she paid her men what she owed them. Usually, she shorted them or refused to pay at all. Her sails were no better than rags, her rigging was frayed and rotten, her plates were rusted beneath her paint, and her captain and chief mate were, now as then, sadists.

She had been Johan Schmidt's first ship, Douglas Victor Hansen his first captain.

The man whose name would become Schmidt had not volunteered.

And now there she was, anchored in the bay, her captain and mate hungry for a crew; desperate for men to haul, and lift, and hoist, and pull; greedy for men to bully, and starve, and beat, and kick, and maim, and cripple, and murder.

"I kill at least one man every trip ... or more," Bully Johnson was said to have once bragged, right there in a Port Townsend saloon. "It discourages the rest of them from starting something I'll have to finish."

Yes, Schmidt thought, they'd need a crew, and therein lay the great opportunity for an enterprising soul such as himself.

However, to help meet that demand, Schmidt would have to recruit a crew of his own. Two men. First one, and then another. He decided to begin with No Ears. Given his relationship with

Big Mike and given the rivalry between Big Mike and Hansen, No Ears seemed like a logical choice.

~~*

Harry "No Ears" Pederson wasn't a hard man to find, especially on a Friday night. On Friday nights, he was usually working behind the bar at the Blue Star Saloon, where he did his best to persuade likely sailors to sign articles without a moment's delay.

Schmidt approached him, and they arranged to talk after closing.

~~*

They talked across a battered table in the barroom, amid the stench of spilled beer and vomit.

"To what do I owe the pleasure?" No Ears asked.

"I need to hire a couple of runners. One night's work. Good money."

No Ears shook his head. "Big Mike wouldn't like that. The town's lousy with crimps as it is."

"I'm trying to do a favor for one of the bank's customers," Schmidt said. "Two guys. One night. There'd be absolutely no threat to Mr. Gamble's interests."

"I don't know," No Ears drawled out. "Why not ask him? Directly like?"

"This has to be done *quietly*. You understand? Too many cooks?"

No Ears nodded. "I get it. Big Mike ain't one to *help*. He likes to run the show."

"Exactly."

"And it won't crowd him?"

"Not at all."

"I see," No Ears said. "Somebody wants somebody out of the way, and somebody else has offered to lend a hand."

Schmidt smiled a conspiratorial smile. "Something like that."

No Ears nodded. "Okay. I know a guy who might be willing to help out."

They agreed to meet again in twenty-four hours on the pier behind the Blue Star Saloon.

~~*

Schmidt was the first to arrive. The pier was dark, lit only by the wash of light from the windows across the back of the Blue Star Saloon. The heft of the Colt in its shoulder holster reassured him. He had, after all, no desire to "volunteer" again.

Two men stepped out of the gloom between the saloon and the next building. The one on the left was No Ears. He introduced the one on the right.

"This here's Charley Ludlow," he said.

Charley was tall, broad through the shoulders and fat through the gut. He smelled like a chamber pot that hasn't been emptied in several days.

"Glad to meet you," Schmidt said.

The two men moved apart.

It was a move that Schmidt had seen many times.

"I tried to tell you Big Mike don't hold with unwelcome competition," No Ears said.

"Yeah," Charley said. He was twitching with anticipation. "He told us to make sure you don't never forget it, neither."

"He said as how a sea voyage might help you remember," No Ears said.

The two men continued to move apart.

Schmidt unbuttoned his suit coat. "No need for that," he said. "I'll go my way, and you can go yours."

"Too late," No Ears said.

"Too bad," Schmidt said, and drew the Colt.

He backed up, sliding his feet behind him, feeling the planking to make sure he didn't trip and go over backwards.

The two men were on opposite sides of him and much, much closer than he would have liked. He ought to have put his back to a wall sooner, but he hadn't. He'd made a mistake, and now that mistake was going to cost him his life.

Maybe.

Schmidt cocked the Colt. "One of you dies," he said.

"Not a chance," Charley said.

And then they were on him.

Schmidt fired, but it came too late. The shot went wide, and a blow hurled the Colt from his hand.

No Ears scooped it up, while Charley kicked Schmidt's legs out from under him.

Schmidt went down.

They kicked him in the stomach, in the ribs, and then in the stomach again.

Charley cocked his foot back.

"Hold on," No Ears said. "Mike told us not to kill him. He ain't no good dead."

"Yeah, right," Charley said, and landed a blow with the side of his boot rather than with the toe.

Schmidt's head snapped to one side. His vision darkened and blurred.

Then came a shot. The flash lit up the pier, the buildings, and the two men. Schmidt saw them as though they were being reflected in funhouse mirrors. The sound slammed off the buildings, tremendous, overpoweringly loud. It rolled like thunder out over the scummy water.

A startled yelp.

Not his.

Then came another shot, deep and loud.

"I got four more in this one and six more in this one."

The sound of drumming boots answered the newcomer's challenge.

The sound faded around the nearest corner.

Schmidt tried to get up but a sharp, hot pain in his ribs stopped him.

A figure knelt down beside him.

"What a miserable way to spend Saturday night. Well, Sunday morning, I suppose," the figure said. It was Clayton McNeill.

"I agree," Schmidt managed to say. "What are you doing here?"

"Saving your miserable hide."

"Thanks," Schmidt said. He could feel himself weakening, suddenly. His body was giving up its hold on consciousness, edging him toward an exhausted collapse. "My revolver. Where is it?"

"Not here."

"I remember No Ears making a grab for it," Schmidt said. "He must have made off with it." And then he could say no more. The effort had become too great.

"All right," Clayton said. "Let's get you home, you damn fool. Didn't you learn anything aboard ship?"

~~*

Schmidt had learned a great deal aboard ship. One of the things he had learned was how to tell the difference between being helped and being taken advantage of. Clayton McNeill was helping.

He sat Schmidt on his bed, pulled his shoes off, took his jacket off, and removed his empty shoulder holster.

"Your shirt's a goner," he said, stating the fact.

"I have others."

"I should hope so, a prosperous bank teller like you."

Clayton cleaned the dirt out of the cut over Schmidt's left eye and washed away as much of the blood as made sense. The rest could wait. They got Schmidt under the covers.

Schmidt asked, "What were you doing down there?"

McNeill made a wry face. "I haven't always been a bookkeeper."

"That's no answer."

McNeill thought for a long time, then he said, "You've been leaving a trail a blind man could follow."

"Trail?"

McNeill arched an eyebrow. "Yes, a *trail*. What you're planning to do, you can't do alone. The rub is you'll need the sort of help you can't hire, not around here, anyway."

"What am I planning to do?"

"Send someone on a sea voyage."

"How do you know that?"

"Hansen isn't dead yet."

THE BANK TELLER

"What are you going to do?"

McNeill thought again, scratched his jaw. "I'd like to throw in with you if you'll have me."

"What have you got against Hansen?"

"Enough."

"Once we cross that line, there'll be no going back."

"What makes you think I haven't already crossed it?"

The room fell silent and the first full light of Sunday morning streamed in through Schmidt's window.

The dinner gong—dinner was served on Sundays—woke the man that Hansen and his mate had signed on as Schmidt. The midday light was bright, and the air drifting in through his window smelled of fir trees and coastal pines.

Schmidt cleaned up as best he could, shaved carefully, changed his shirt, and went down to the kitchen. He was far too late to be seated in the dining room. The cook took pity on him and gave him more than a late-comer's due.

As he ate, he thought back through the mistakes he had made, reviewed the lessons he had learned in the *Shattuck*'s forecastle and on her decks. They were good lessons, ones he vowed never to ignore again. Over his coffee, he decided to retrieve his Colt.

But before he could accomplish that laudable task, he had two items to buy. One of which he should have bought the moment he'd landed in Seattle. In truth it had been his vanity and not his desire for anonymity that had stopped him.

~~*

THE GREAT MYSTERY OF ETERNITY

The Quimper Mercantile and Chandlery was open for business on Sundays.

It was the task of a few minutes to purchase a derringer, a box of cartridges, and an ebony-wood cane. The cane wasn't a belaying pin, but it would do for the likes of Harry "No Ears" Pederson.

~~*

No Ears was a man of neither regular employment nor regular habits, but he did have one fixed point in his routine. On Sundays, when he could afford to, he ate supper at Mrs. Chang's Chowder and Oyster Bar. After which, he would cross back over to the Blue Star and do whatever Big Mike had in store for him.

Today, however, No Ears cut around the rear of Chang's and headed for the Northern Lights Hotel, the best brothel in Port Townsend. His route took him down Sherman's Alley, which had a sharp dogleg that sheltered it from Water Street.

Schmidt sprang from a gap between the buildings and surged up behind No Ears. Before No Ears could swing around, Schmidt brought his ebony-wood cane down and across onto the man's thigh. He brought it down hard and fast.

No Ears yelled and collapsed into the slurry of horse-dung and mud that served as the alley's pavement. His eyes were wild, his face twisted in pain. He was gasping and moaning. His breath was foul with the stench of clam chowder and decaying teeth.

Schmidt planted the heel of his shoe on the man's neck, hard enough to mean business. "Where's my revolver?" Schmidt asked.

"I sold it."

Schmidt twisted his heel. "No, you didn't. You'd keep a gun

THE BANK TELLER

like that." He lifted the cane, readying it. "Where's my gun?"

"Honest. I sold it."

Schmidt drew his new derringer and cocked it. He aimed it at the other man's face.

"To whom?"

"A guy. He came into the Blue Star and we got to talking about guns. You know how it is. I sold it to him."

"Who is he?"

"I don't know. Logger, I guess."

"I want my gun back." Schmidt pressed harder with his heel. He increased the pressure until No Ears squealed like a pig and started coughing. "Find it."

No Ears nodded as vigorously as he could with the side of his face pressed into a pile of horse dung. "Yes, sir. As soon as I can."

"Sooner than that, my friend. Much sooner," Schmidt said, and stepped away, releasing him.

No Ears didn't say a word, but rubbed his neck and scrambled off down the alley.

Schmidt watched him until he disappeared around a corner, then Schmidt turned and headed for Water Street. He had nothing to do until he showed up for work on Monday morning.

~~*

Shortly before the bank opened its doors on Monday morning, Clayton McNeill came over to Schmidt's teller's cage. He was carrying a neatly folded newspaper.

"You have any interest in the *Susan B. Shattuck*?"

"What about her?" Schmidt asked.

McNeill handed him the paper. "Interesting piece about her," he said, and moved away.

The shipping column reported the *Shattuck* was scheduled to sail on Wednesday morning for Suva. Her cargo consisted of lumber and balks of timber.

Which meant that every crimp in Port Townsend, including Hansen, would be scouring Water Street on Tuesday night. The beer and the hard stuff, together with the chloral hydrate and the laudanum, would be flowing like the runoff from a monsoon.

Under those conditions, two extra men were hardly likely to attract attention.

After supper on Tuesday, Mr. Schmidt and Mr. McNeill joined Mrs. Abbott and Mr. Kearney, a school teacher, for a game of whist. At nine o'clock, they excused themselves and went to their rooms. By half past nine, they were on Water Street, and by ten o'clock, they were crouched among the pilings beneath the Mariner's Rest, Hansen's boarding house. They had their guns drawn. Schmidt held his derringer in his left hand, his cane at the ready in his right.

Sooner or later, unaware of what he was doing, Hansen would come to them.

All they had to do was wait ... in the dark and the cold—wait and listen to the raucous voices filtering down from the rooming house above them, listen to the gentle thud of a rowboat as it rocked against Hansen's neatly ordered dock.

~~*

THE BANK TELLER

Their wait was over before Schmidt's leg had stiffened in the cold.

At ten thirty, Hansen and two of his runners descended the stairs that lead down from a trapdoor in one of the backrooms. Hansen was in the lead, dressed in a business suit and a derby hat.

His two runners were half dragging and half carrying a man between them. He was Harry "No Ears" Pederson. His hands were tied behind his back, and he looked decidedly the worse for whatever it was he'd been drinking. He was mumbling semi-coherently about how he'd get even with them someday.

"Shut up," one of the runners said, and thumped No Ears on the back of the head with a sap.

No Ears let out a long, agonized sigh and sagged.

"Now look at what you've done," the second runner said.

"Shut up, the two of you," Hansen said. "Get him into the boat and be quick about it. Burgess is waiting."

The first runner said, "Yeah, Burgess and Burgess's money."

"With lots more where that's coming from," the second runner said.

The first runner pointed at No Ears. "And lots more where *that* came from."

The three of them shared a hearty laugh and manhandled No Ears toward the boat. They set him down, and the first runner climbed into the boat.

They had No Ears straddled between the boat and the dock when Schmidt and McNeill charged out of the gloom.

Their attack was fast, but it wasn't instantaneous. Hansen had time to turn, his face wide with shock. He thrust his hand beneath his suit jacket.

McNeill shouldered the second runner, the one who'd stayed

on the dock, into Hansen, throwing him backwards.

The runner bounced off his boss, stumbled, caught his foot on the bullrail, and pitched over the edge. He hit his head on the boat's gunwale and ended up flailing in the filth-choked water, stunned and disoriented.

No Ears dropped onto the planking like a sack of weevil-infested flour. He lay there, breathing but otherwise inert.

By this time, Hansen's gun had cleared. For all the good it did him.

Schmidt brought his ebony cane down on Hansen's forearm, a vicious, snapping blow.

Hansen's hand jerked open and his gun—a nickel-plated showpiece—flew into the water. His mouth opened in a startled gasp.

"Hurts, doesn't it?" Schmidt said.

The first runner, the one in the boat, had his gun out. It was a small-caliber pocket pistol, also nickel-plated, more a piece of jewelry than anything else. He fired several times, but because he was panicked and because the boat was rocking, the shots went wild. The slugs hit pilings and joists and the mud at the edge of the water.

McNeill leveled his gun at the man's forehead.

"That's enough, Sammy. Behave or I'll blow your head off."

Sammy nodded.

"Ditch the gun."

Sammy looked pained. "Aw, gee, Mr. McNeill, I just bought it. Took me months to save up for it."

"Too bad," McNeill said. "Do it."

Sammy gazed lovingly at his gun, but then he dropped it overboard.

THE BANK TELLER

Hansen said, "You here to get a little of your own back, are you, Clay?"

"Call it a down payment," McNeill said.

"I had a hunch you'd turn on me someday."

"You should have paid it more heed."

The drumming of heavy boots sounded from the planks over their heads. Sammy's shots had attracted someone's attention.

Schmidt said, "We're running out of time."

~~*

Five minutes later, No Ears was fumbling his way back toward Water Street and freedom. Out on the water, Hansen and his two runners sat tied up in the rowboat, while McNeill and Schmidt rowed away from the pier.

The minutes ticked silently by.

When they were no scant distance out in the bay, Schmidt and McNeill stopped rowing.

McNeill drew his gun and trained it on the three captives.

"This where you're gonna kill us?" Hansen asked.

"No," Schmidt said. "This is where I'm gonna offer to buy you boys a drink." Schmidt produced a pint bottle and pulled the cork. "You can drink it," he said, "or we can force it down your throats. Your choice."

The three men drank, round after round until they'd drained the bottle. Then, thanks to the chloral hydrate, they passed out, making an irregular heap. They looked like nothing quite so much as a pile of garbage.

Schmidt and McNeill gripped their oars and resumed rowing.

Ahead of them lay the *Susan B. Shattuck*. She was tall, and graceful, and outmoded, and stunningly beautiful in the starlight.

~~*

By the time the bank opened on Wednesday morning, the *Shattuck* was a memory.

By the time the bank opened on Thursday morning, the news had spread up and down Water Street that Captain Hansen and two of his goons had gone missing. The police said that it was too early to declare him missing. Like as not, he'd taken the steamer over to Seattle. His employees said otherwise.

Shortly before closing on Friday, Harry "No Ears" Pederson presented himself at Schmidt's window.

"Good afternoon, Mr. Pederson," Schmidt said. He smiled warmly. "May I help you?"

"Hello, Mr. Schmidt," No Ears said. "I wanted to thank you for what you done for me. I'd have been halfway to China by now if it hadn't been for you."

"Thanks, but I don't have the vaguest idea what you're talking about."

No Ears wasn't stupid. "Then I must have you confused with somebody else."

"I'm sure of it," Schmidt said.

No Ears set a box about the size of book on the counter. He slid it across toward Schmidt. "I believe this belongs to you."

"What have we here?" Schmidt asked, and carefully opened the box. Inside, nestled in a wrapping of oiled brown paper, was his Colt revolver. It had been cleaned to a bright shine and freshly oiled. "Thank you very much, Mr. Pederson. I won't forget."

"Are we square?"

THE BANK TELLER

"Yes, we're square."

Pederson nodded and hurried from the bank.

Schmidt placed the box in a drawer.

McNeill approached and said, "He returned your revolver?"

"He did."

"That was considerate of him."

"I suspect it's because he isn't on his way to Suva."

"Come on, Smitty. He would have had to have hocked his shoelaces to buy it back. How'd you convince him to do it?"

Schmidt said, "Well, I haven't always been a banker."

THE RABBI, THE VAMPIRE, AND THE MITZVOT

> *An observant Jew who is also a recently turned vampire faces many challenges, not the least of which is finding a rabbi who works nights.*

IN THE WELL-TENDED COURTYARD of the synagogue the security lamps made the night as bright as a heavily overcast day, but around the young man at the bottom of his office steps, Rabbi Michael Rosenbaum imagined he could see a wash of shadow, not just around his feet but on all sides, below and above. It appeared as though the night, comforting and protective, had draped itself around the young man.

Was it a trick of the light? A burned out bulb in the porch fixture? An effect of the young man's clothes, which were gray and black? As if he had attempted to balance the somber colors, he wore a bright green-and-white scarf, white running shoes, and a kippah that would have rivaled Jacob's coat. Who was he, this late-night visitor, this tall, thin, angular goth lookalike, this post-adolescent dressed for an avant-garde funeral?

"Good evening," the rabbi said.

"Can you help me?" the young man asked.

Rabbi Rosenbaum resettled his grip on his briefcase. "I'm on my way home. Is it an emergency? Can you come back in the morning?"

The young man looked down toward his feet, then back up at the rabbi. His eyes were dark, as dark as almost everything else about him. "Yes, it's an emergency, but no, I can't come back ... in the morning."

Marvelous, the rabbi groused to himself. "So, what's this emergency of yours?"

The young man stepped forward. His face would have been dark-complected, like that of someone from a Middle-Eastern country, except that it had paled significantly. As faces went, it looked as though it ought to belong to a dying general in an eighteenth-century painting of a battle.

"I'm starving to death," the young man said. "No joke, I might die, as in dead dead. That kind of die."

With all the feeding programs and soup kitchens there were in operation, Rabbi Rosenbaum found this an odd claim; but being a generous man, the rabbi reached for his wallet. "I don't have a lot of cash with me, but—"

"No, it isn't a question of money," the young man said. "Please, Rabbi, I need to talk to you. I'm not a thug or anything. I promise I won't hurt you."

Rabbi Rosenbaum made a dismissive gesture. "The thought never crossed my mind."

And indeed it hadn't. After twenty-five years in northwest Portland, Oregon, through good times and bad, he had developed a sense of who might pose a danger and who probably did not, a sense of those who begged to buy food and those who begged to buy alcohol or drugs. Now that the picture had begun to build up, he could tell that this unusual young man fell into another category: the confused, the anxious, the fearful.

The rabbi's wife and family, not to mention his dinner, late though it already was, could wait another few minutes. By now it would need to be microwaved, anyway.

THE RABBI, THE VAMPIRE, AND THE MITZVOT

Rabbi Rosenbaum reopened the door. "Come in. We can talk in my office."

He led the way through the reception area, where his secretary worked, and on into his office. He switched on the lights and pointed his guest toward the brace of chairs in front of the desk. "Would you care for tea? Coffee? I can make either."

The young man shrugged. "I'll have whatever you're having."

"Coffee, then. I'm a little weary of tea."

After the water had started to trickle through the coffee grounds, Rabbi Rosenbaum sat down behind his desk. Secretly, he was glad for the distance, the separation it provided. The young man seemed safe enough, but who could tell for certain?

The rabbi asked, "What brings you to me? What about your own rabbi? You are Jewish, aren't you?"

Rabbi Rosenbaum sounded to himself like one of those bores at parties who shoots out questions like a machine gun, never waiting for an answer. Still, anyone could put a kippah on his head—not that it could make any difference in the outcome to a plea for help.

The young man wrung his hands together, whitening the knuckles. "Yes, I'm Jewish. Orthodox in fact. Observant." His words cascaded out, like a row of falling dominoes, each one eager to push over its neighbor. "Or I was Jewish. Before. Maybe I still am. I must be. I'm not dead, not exactly; and even if I were, I'd still be Jewish if I existed at all. Once a Jew always a Jew. If you catch my drift."

Rabbi Rosenbaum decided to follow this new thread: '... not dead, not exactly.' What had his guest meant by that? Was he dying? In an attempt to edge up to the real topic, the rabbi said, "You know who I am, but I don't know who you are."

"No reason you should. I'm Simeon Black. I went to *shul* at the Willamette Falls Jewish Center."

The coffeemaker made a sputtering hiss, and the rabbi went to attend to it.

When they had their coffees, the rabbi said, "You often speak of yourself in the past tense. I once knew a man who adopted a similar habit after he learned he had cancer."

The rabbi tasted his coffee. It was too weak—*dreck* in fact--and had a strange flavor, as though the roaster had ground a batch of flavored coffee before grinding the rabbi's order.

"Cancer—I should be so lucky," Simeon said. "It would make my existence a whole lot easier."

A spark of genuine concern flashed in the rabbi's mind. "They're your feelings, of course, and we've all had them, but life is too great a blessing to wish for death."

"That's just it, Rabbi, I'm not alive and I'm not dead."

A burst of anger, of hurt, hit Rabbi Rosenbaum. He had no intention of sitting still for what he could so easily guess was coming. This young man, this Simeon Black, if that was his real name, had suckered him.

But just in case he hadn't, the rabbi asked, "What do you mean?"

"I mean I'm one of the undead. I'm a vampire, a fanger."

~~*

Because he was a Conservative Jew with leanings toward Orthodoxy, Rabbi Michael Rosenbaum lived within an easy walk of his synagogue. Leaving his office, he headed up Vaughn Street, crossed 21st, and turned south onto 23rd.

THE RABBI, THE VAMPIRE, AND THE MITZVOT

Farther along the street than he had to go, fashionable shops and restaurants lined the avenue; but in this section, the neighborhood still held an echo of the working-class, bohemian character he'd enjoyed so much before northwest Portland had transformed itself into a fashionable success.

He glanced at his watch: 10:17. He'd have to scrounge dinner from the leftovers in the refrigerator and nuke them in the microwave if he wanted them hot. The children would be in bed, and his wife would be curled up with a book. Only his dogs, Goniff and Schnorrer—a Golden Retriever and a Doberman—would come to the door to greet him.

Was he feeling sorry for himself? Yes, perhaps a little, but after Simeon Black's strange visit and after his terrible mishandling of it, a profound sense of discontent had overtaken him, like a pack of wolves bringing down an unwary ungulate.

Of all the horrific things that mental illness could do to a person, perhaps the unremitting loneliness that it imposed was the most devastating. Easily, it could be the most dangerous. It threw the sufferer down from circle to circle, like a Slinky, until he crashed onto the ice at the very bottom of Dante's image of hell, where he thrashed and twisted until he had embedded himself in the ice of his own terror.

Fr. David Lloyd, one of the rabbi's few friends among the neighborhood Christian clergy, loved to cite that haunting spectacle. He loved to point out that in Dante's hell the worst punishment of all is to be frozen in emotional and spiritual sterility. Dante places Satan not in a lake of fire but in a prison of ice.

As the rabbi crossed Upshur, a bag lady pushed her shopping cart out of an alley and onto the sidewalk. With a loud grunt, she heaved the cart around and started it toward him.

She had piled the basket with white and brown plastic shopping bags, and the ones tied around the rim had labels on them: living room, bedroom, bathroom, and kitchen.

The woman had covered her clothes in layers of bags. She wore white kitchen bags, black garbage bags, and the stiff, multicolored shopping bags.

The rabbi couldn't embarrass her or diminish himself by crossing the street, but as the distance between them shrank, the odors of stale urine and human feces assaulted him. The woman smelled as though she had messed her pants hours ago and hadn't bothered to clean herself up. She didn't gibber; rather, she hummed the melody to the "Ode to Joy" from Beethoven's 9th Symphony.

When they had drawn to within a few feet of each other, the humming stopped. Her eyes, sharp and cold, sent a shiver down the rabbi's spine. He'd never before seen eyes like hers on a human being. They were the eyes of a perfect predator. And yet, within their depths, he could see a shattering loneliness.

Funny, that he should have just been pondering that sort of isolation.

Unsure of his intent—whether to offer her aid or to salve his own conscience—he offered her a ten-dollar bill.

"I don't want your charity," she said.

Hers was not the voice of a homeless alcoholic or drug addict.

"Then call it a loan. Pay me back when you can."

She stared at the bill. "No, I don't want it."

He edged the bill closer to her. "Please. Accept it as a favor to me."

"All right, but I'll pay it back. I will, you know. I promise you, Rabbi."

THE RABBI, THE VAMPIRE, AND THE MITZVOT

She took the bill, wormed it between the folds of her garbage bags and thrust it deep into what he assumed was a coat pocket.

She resumed her humming and went on down the street, heading north. Her humming grew in power, further, further, until suddenly it had transformed into Beethoven's magnificent music. It filled the street, the spaces between the buildings, her clear, unforced, *impossible* soprano.

He listened until she turned east onto Vaughn and the music faded.

An unexpected moment of fear tore at him. He'd never seen her before, and he hadn't introduced himself. How had she known he was a rabbi?

~~*

Over the telephone, the rabbi's closest friend, Dr. Levy Shapiro, said, "... and then he told you he was a vampire. How did you handle it?"

"Not very well, I'm afraid. I threw him out and went home. I worried all night. What if it wasn't a sick prank? What if that young man actually believes he's a vampire? There's no telling what he might do."

"Psychosis, sexual perversion, or prank. Is that how you see it?"

"What else could it be?"

"Nothing," Levy said. "So-called vampirism is quite the rage these days. I treated two cases last month. Did you call Willamette Falls?"

"Yes, first thing this morning. They know a Simeon Black, but no one's seen him in a few days. Anyway, Levy, that doesn't prove a thing. My visitor could have found the name in a telephone book and decided to use it."

"Listen to me, you did the right thing. If he's psychotic, sooner or later, he'll find help, maybe not thanks to you, but he will find it. Anyway, you're not qualified to deal with the undead; as a psychiatrist, I am. Dollars to doughnuts, you'll never see him again."

~~*

But Rabbi Rosenbaum did see him again.

As he had the night before, the man who'd called himself Simeon Black stood in a pool of shadow outside the office when the rabbi left for home at the end of yet another long day.

After the mutual recriminations and apologies, the rabbi asked for an explanation.

In answer, the young man opened his mouth, pulled back his upper lip, and ran out his canine teeth. At full extension, they were about half as long as his index fingers. They glistened a brilliant white in the security lights.

"Where do you think I got these? Moe Greenberg's Costume Shop?" He ran his canines in and out a few times for emphasis. "Or maybe I hunted up a demented denturist and paid him to install them for me, complete with the hydraulics."

"We'd better talk inside," the rabbi said.

"Sure. Got any more coffee? And maybe a little vodka to go with it?"

When they had their drinks and had seated themselves—the rabbi sat behind his desk and Simeon took one of the chairs across from him—the rabbi asked, "What happened? How did you ...?"

THE RABBI, THE VAMPIRE, AND THE MITZVOT

"The ugliest, filthiest woman I've ever seen jumped me on my way home a few nights ago." He pulled his scarf and shirt collar aside, exposing two puncture wounds, well along toward healing, on the side of his neck. "See what she did to me?" he asked. "To make a long story short, the next morning, I woke up feeling really strange. I called in sick and decided to go for a walk. The minute I opened the door, the direct sunlight struck my hand. Thank God that's all it struck!"

He held up his left hand. Angry blisters, which were, however, well along toward healing, carpeted the skin.

"Someone playing games with a laser?" the rabbi asked.

"Nice try, but that doesn't explain the bite marks or the fangs."

"No, it doesn't."

The rabbi topped off their coffees with more vodka. To him, it seemed to be the sort of night that called for more vodka. "Out of morbid curiosity, how do your fangs work? They're for tearing open the throat, I suppose."

Simeon laughed. "That's what most people think, but, no, they're not. They're more like two honking soda straws." He set a small, hand-bound book on the desk. "According to that, they connect, via several new organs I didn't have before, into my circulatory system. Slashing open someone's throat and drinking their blood wouldn't do me any good at all."

The rabbi picked up the book: *So Now You've Become a Vampire, A Guide for the Newly Turned* by Ima Blutsauger. "Where'd this come from?"

"From under my doormat. A few minutes after I'd fried my hand, the phone rings. It's a woman. She says, 'You weren't supposed to happen, but I couldn't let you die.' Then, 'I left you something under your mat. Learn it, love it, undead it. Remember, no direct sunlight.' As soon as it was dusk, I went out and turned over my doormat. And there it was, that book."

Gesturing with it, the rabbi said, "May I borrow this for a day or two? I'd like to read it."

"Sure. I've already made a photocopy. Backups. You know."

The rabbi set the book off to one side. From here on out, it was going to be a question of approach, of how best to work within Simeon's beliefs about himself without losing track of objective reality. After all, any costume shop worth its salt could come up with fangs every bit as convincing. "What can I do for you?"

"I told you I was observant. *Am* observant. Was observant? Sorry, I'm having trouble with the grammar. What do you think?"

"You seem to me to be very alive. By your own admission you're not dead. That's what undead means, doesn't it? If you're not dead, you must be alive, at least in some sense of the word. Use the present tense."

"You make a lot of sense. I'm glad I came to you. Well, Rabbi, the question is, how does an observant Jewish vampire keep kosher?"

~~*

The telephone crackled for a moment in the rabbi's ear, and then Moe Greenberg, the owner of Moe Greenberg's Costume Shop, said, "Here they are. Looks like I carry a couple of different brands of vampire fangs, but not ones that grow."

"Are they available?"

"I don't see why not. You could always have a set made. I know a guy in L.A. who could run up a set for you."

THE RABBI, THE VAMPIRE, AND THE MITZVOT

The rabbi thanked Moe for his help and called Levy Shapiro.

"How's your vampire?" Levy asked.

"He's why I called. He wants me to tell him how he can keep kosher."

Levy guffawed. "You're kidding!"

"No, not at all. He's quite worried about it."

"But vampires drink blood."

"Hence his dilemma," the rabbi said. "He may as well be asking me how to make kosher bacon."

"Let me know if you figure it out. I grew up eating bacon. By the way, what did you tell him?"

"That I had to think about it."

"Good answer."

"About my vampire," the rabbi said, "would he go so far as to make himself a set of mechanical fangs?"

"How far will a psychotic go to reinforce his psychosis? How high is up?" There was a pause, then, "Or are you asking me whether you've stumbled across a live one?"

The rabbi hadn't considered that interpretation of his question. He chuckled. "I see what you mean, but no, I haven't. I didn't think it through. His fangs are quite ingenious, though. They work like a car's radio antenna, only instead of going up and down, they go down and up."

Another pause from Levy, then, "Look, my next appointment is here. Quickly, does your vampire pose a danger to himself or others?"

Rabbi Rosenbaum thought about it. "No, I don't think so. He's confused and he's frightened, but he's not dangerous."

"Then we can't do much for him until he either does pose a danger or asks for our help. In the meantime, play along and keep an eye on him. But be careful. Psychotics can turn vicious in a heartbeat."

"I'm not worried."

"You should be."

~~*

Ugly gray swatches had formed beneath Simeon Black's eyes and his cheeks were sunken.

Rabbi Rosenbaum said, "You look as though you may be ill."

"I haven't eaten since I was turned."

"Nothing at all?"

"Water, soda, coffee—that sort of thing. No blood."

The rabbi felt a cold ball form in the pit of his stomach. "I see." But he knew, of course, that he didn't.

Simeon poured a healthy splash of vodka into his tea, sweetened it with two cubes of sugar, and drank off half the cup in one go. "You know what worries me the most, on the mundane side? How do I have my teeth cleaned?"

Simeon was smiling, so the rabbi allowed himself to chuckle.

"We're having a good laugh, but think about it. Even assuming I can find a dentist's office that's open nights, they're bound to take X-rays." He pointed to where his fangs supposedly rested in his upper jaw. "What happens when these babies show up on the film? They'll freak. That's what."

The rabbi let him talk on without interruption, nodding now and then to show his understanding.

"And I'll need a different job. There's lots of night work, but how do I show up between eight and five for the interviews and to fill out the paperwork? What if they want a urine sample for a drug screen? God only knows what's floating around in mine or what they'll do when they find it. And what about banking? First National Vampires of America? I don't think so."

The rabbi sipped his tea. "Make do. Even in a city as provincial as Portland, you ought to be able to find alternatives."

Simeon leaned back in his chair. "Enough *kvetching*." A hunted look came into his eyes. "You know what flat out scares me? That woman, the one who bit me—filthy, dressed in rags, the deranged desperation in her eyes. I've always been afraid of poverty, but now I have a fresh horror. It's of ending up like her. She did this to me and all I can think about is how miserable she must be, existing as a pathetic monster; and how I don't want to end up like her. She smelled like the sewer line coming out of a slaughter house."

The rabbi remembered how he had forced himself to stay on the same side of the street with that bag lady a few days ago. It was bad enough to be anywhere near that degree of filth, but to live that way ...

Simeon shook his head back and forth. "I'd rather be dead, not undead, but dead dead."

"I understand," the rabbi said, "but I don't believe those fears constitute the worst of your nightmares."

Simeon refilled his cup with tea and vodka, in roughly equal measures. He was far from drunk, but his eyes had a glassy, fevered sheen—not enough food, too little sleep, too much sugar, too much caffeine.

"Then what does?" Simeon asked.

"The prospect of standing as an abomination before God."

"How—"

"Your worry about *kashrut* betrays your true fear. You want to observe, but you can't. You're trapped. Sooner or later, you'll have to take an innocent life in order to stay alive, but murder is a sin. Yet, if you don't, you'll die at your own hand, as it were—another sin. You might argue that you've become a malign predator and that you'd be killing yourself in order to save others, but such an argument rings a trifle hollow. To kill a genuine predator, an animal that kills only to stay alive—as, sooner or later, you will—is yet another grave sin. Why? Because in killing for food the predator obeys his God-given nature. He *is* innocent."

"But am I not obliged to kill the predators who threaten my family or my stock?"

"No, you're obliged only to protect your family and your stock. You're under no obligation to kill."

"And what if killing is the only way?"

"The point can be argued in dozens of different ways, but I'd venture there's almost always an alternative to killing. On the other hand, if there weren't, then killing would be justified." Taking a gamble, the rabbi said, "Simeon, I can't tell you it's lawful for you to kill yourself."

"And you're not even warmed up yet," Simeon said, smiling.

The rabbi felt his face flush. "I'm barely started, in fact." He tried to distill his thoughts into a practical piece of advice, but without success. He said, "The point is that shades of gray, choices between evils, encompass you like the stone walls of a prison, and above it all, making your situation intolerable, stands your desire to obey the commandments of God, the *mitzvot*."

"I'm not in a prison, and I don't want to escape; I want to observe."

"Must you kill your, well, prey?"

"I can't leave a trail of witnesses. I'd betray myself and every other vampire in the region. I'd be as good as committing suicide *and* murdering them."

The rabbi thought it over. "I see your argument, but what about the bite marks on the corpses?"

"I don't know. Yet. Maybe by the time they're found, enough of the soft tissue has rotted away that—" He stopped, then said, "My God, we sound like we're trying to figure out what happens to used motor oil. What kind of a monster am I?"

"The frightened kind."

Simeon drank his tea. He laid his head back against the chair. "To tell you the truth, Rabbi, I feel like shit," he said. "So, what's your answer? How can I feed and keep kosher? This isn't like eating a cheese burger because you don't want to embarrass a well-meaning but unknowledgeable gentile host."

"No, it's not." The rabbi carefully thought through what he wanted to say and how he wanted to say it. He had several paths to follow, but in the end, he chose first principles, or as close to them as he figured he needed to be. After all, Simeon believed in God, believed that God had chosen the Jews to be His people, believed that He had given them commandments, those 613 *mitzvot*, to make them holy, believed that the commandments bound them. But Simeon, in his devotion to God, in his confusion and terror at what he believed had happened to him, had forgotten that the Lord is just.

"How do you, a vampire, keep kosher? You don't. For you, *kashrut* doesn't apply."

Simeon's eyes went wide. "Why not? I'm a Jew."

"Yes, you are, but the *mitzvot* presuppose the ability to comply. You cannot comply with *kashrut* without committing suicide. Therefore, you're exempt."

Simeon made a face. "That's too glib, but let's say I'm convinced. What about the matter of committing murder every time I feed?"

"Ah, well, there we face a possibly less tractable problem."

"Not if you're the victim. Not if you're the murderer."

"I didn't say I had the answer. Not yet, anyway." The Rabbi thought, then asked, "What about animal blood? Would that work?"

Simeon's face lit up but not by much. "According to Blutsauger, it might work for a while."

"Then I'd suggest you try it until we can figure something out."

"What kind of animals?"

Another problem without a strict solution. "The ones that can be kashered if a shohet slaughters them properly: cows, sheep, chickens, not pigs, not shellfish. You know the list as well as I do. They must die as painlessly as possible, and so on."

"That's all well and good, Rabbi," Simeon said desperately, "but sooner or later, I'll have to feed on another human being or I'll have to kill myself to ensure that I don't."

~~*

Levy Shapiro asked, "Does he pose an imminent danger to himself or others?"

"Yes, I believe he does," Rabbi Rosenbaum said. "We might have a couple of days before he acts but no longer."

"Fine. We'll need to have him admitted to a psych ward for observation."

"Without his consent?"

"Maybe. The laws are tangled in this area, but I think I can

THE RABBI, THE VAMPIRE, AND THE MITZVOT

find a judge who'll sign an order."

That night, Simeon Black returned to the rabbi's office at nine o'clock. At nine-fifteen, Levy Shapiro stunned him with a Taser and followed up by injecting him with enough sedative to knock out three men his size. By ten-thirty, Simeon was sleeping it off in Room 24 on the psych floor of St. Luke's Hospital.

On their way off the floor, Rabbi Rosenbaum asked the charge nurse to keep the draperies in Simeon's room tightly drawn.

"Why's that?"

"He has a horror of sunlight," the rabbi said.

The nurse turned to Levy Shapiro, her eyebrows raised in a silent question.

"Yes, keep the draperies closed. It's an excellent idea. Thank you for reminding me, Rabbi."

Rabbi Rosenbaum shrugged, dismissing the compliment. There had been enough betrayals for one night, and there was absolutely no point in adding another—the betrayal of not taking Simeon Black's fears seriously—to the list, especially when such an addition would amount to no more than an act of wanton cruelty.

~~*

The next day, in the morning, the nurse buzzed the rabbi and the doctor onto the psych floor a little before sunrise.

In response to Levy's question, the nurse at the nurses' station checked a chart. "Mr. Black awoke at 2:35. He became agitated and demanded to be released. His situation was explained to him and he agreed to discuss it with you today. Since then, he's been resting quietly."

She handed Levy the chart, he scanned it, and returned it to her.

"How is he now?" Levy asked.

"No one's been down to check on him in the last hour," the nurse said. "We've had a hazardous materials incident."

"What sort of incident?" Levy asked.

"Something contaminated the ventilation system, Dr. Shapiro. Paint fumes, I think. A hazmat team came up and checked all of the rooms on the floor."

"When?"

"They left a half hour ago. We're only now bringing things back under control."

Shapiro's jaw flexed, and as if in sympathetic response, the rabbi felt the muscles around his mouth tighten. He willed them to relax. Showing his concern would only make the situation worse. Besides, there really wasn't anything to be concerned about. Simeon Black was resting in his room, and it wasn't as though the nurses and orderlies had decided to throw a wild party. They'd been busy with the hazardous-materials team.

"Thank you," Levy said. "I'll look in on my patient now."

Levy and the rabbi walked down the corridor toward Room 24.

Orderlies and nurses hurried up and down, and the television in the day room played a news program. The murmuring of one of the patients and the shrill, horrified complaints of another about men from Jupiter in white space suits competed with a weather report for the Mid-Atlantic States. All the while a pervasive sense of ill-contained chaos lent a paradoxical measure of structure to the atmosphere on the floor.

The rabbi asked, "Who runs this place, Mitch Oohganer?"

"Very funny," Levy said. "They have their problems, but they run the best psych floor in Portland."

Fine, but just how much was that saying? Rather than express his skepticism, the rabbi said, "Sorry. I didn't mean to criticize."

Rabbi Rosenbaum had, of course, visited patients on other psych floors and on this one, but each time he did, he experienced the same reactions: revulsion, an irrational fear for his safety, and an overwhelming need to make bad jokes. No matter how many visits he made—and they had become evermore frequent in recent years—he could never develop a thick-enough skin about them. Professional detachment? What a joke!

He'd also never mastered nursing homes and pediatric-oncology wards.

He hoped he never would. He promised himself that if he ever did, if he ever became that callus, he'd quit serving a congregation and go into selling shoes.

Because the hospital ran north and south, the rooms faced either east, toward Mt. Hood, or west, toward the West Hills. Twenty-four faced east.

A sick feeling coursed through the rabbi's stomach, as though he'd gulped down too much strong coffee. He'd remembered about the drapes, but how could he have forgotten about the orientation of the room itself?

When they were still some steps away, an orderly said, "You're here to see Room 24, aren't you?"

"Yes, we are," Levy said.

As though he were divulging a secret, the orderly said, "Once he settled down, he had a good night. He slept right through the hazmat team's visit."

"Oh?" the rabbi asked. "Did they create a disturbance?"

"They always do," the orderly said, "running around in those suits of theirs, barking orders like they were out on maneuvers. They scared the crap out of a lot of the patients." He gave them a wry grin. "I know 'cause I had to clean 'em up."

A shriek came from the day room, and the orderly hurried away.

Levy Shapiro and Rabbi Rosenbaum resumed their trek toward Room 24.

They had reached Room 20 when a loud *WHOOMP* and the sound of shattering glass came from behind the door to Room 24. A flash like a strobe light firing stabbed out around the door, and the fire alarm went off.

They ran the few remaining steps to the door.

"You don't dare open it," the rabbi said.

Levy pressed his hand to the door. "It's cold," he said, as though that meaningless piece of information gave him permission to do anything he wanted to. He pushed open the door.

Water sprayed from the automatic sprinkler heads in the ceiling, fogging the room. Already the spent water had formed into puddles on the floor. Someone had opened the drapes and bright sunlight flooded in. Like the beam of a spotlight, it struck the bed. Along it lay a thick, man-shaped layer of ash. The bedclothes had charred, and small fires burned everywhere. Even the paint on the chairs was smoldering.

On the nightstand, the remains of a clock radio bubbled and crackled and sent up a trail of foul-smelling smoke.

The rabbi fell back against the door frame. "My God," he whispered. "He really—"

But he choked off the rest. He stumbled out into the hallway, staggered a few paces down it, and collapsed against a wall. His throat tightened, his nose stung, and he felt tears overflow his eyes and run down his face.

Whatever Simeon Black may have been, he had come to the rabbi for help, and rather than help him, rather than believe the evidence of his own eyes, one way or another, he had driven that unfortunate man to a hideous death.

Did it matter who had opened the drapes, a careless orderly or Simeon Black himself? No less than any vampire, Rabbi Rosenbaum had followed his nature and death had resulted. Just as much as any of them, he, too, had turned into a killer.

And so he wept, there in the hallway, amid the screaming patients, the blaring fire alarm, the shouting staff, and the metallic rush of the sprinklers.

~~*

A few days later, Levy Shapiro telephoned Rabbi Rosenbaum at the synagogue.

"The authorities have ruled that Simeon Black's death was an accident," Levy said. "The hospital is calling it a freakish tragedy."

The good doctor went on to explain. Once upon a time, the floor that was now the psych floor had contained ordinary patient rooms, and each, naturally, had been equipped with an oxygen feed. When the floor had been converted to psychiatric use, the contractors had removed the oxygen feeds and had capped and plastered over the lines, but they had not removed the lines themselves from the walls. It made sense at the time. After all, the floor might be converted back to strictly medical use. Evidently, one of those lines had developed a leak and had filled

Simeon Black's room with oxygen while he slept. The first electrical spark that had come along had set the whole thing off like a fuel-air bomb.

Finishing up, Levy said, "Oxygen can be wicked."

Not as wicked as we can, the rabbi thought. He asked, "What about the hazardous-materials incident?"

"Reviewed ad nauseam. Perfectly legitimate. Sorry, but our wannabe vampire was accidentally immolated."

Even without the knowledge that Simeon Black had been a vampire, the hospital's explanation for what had happened in Room 24 had more holes in it than the walls of a termite-infested house.

But Rabbi Rosenbaum chose to let it go. If he pursued the matter, he could only end up answering a string of very uncomfortable questions with equally ludicrous answers.

He could practically hear the gossip. "Say, Danny, did you hear about Rabbi Rosenbaum. He went *meshugeh*. He imagined he'd met a vampire, who—Get this!—wanted to keep kosher! Have you ever in your life heard of such a thing. No, of course, not. No one has. And so what does our beloved rabbi do? He tried to help! He tried to help a creature of darkness and evil! Can you imagine! What a *schmendrick*!"

~~*

The young woman stood in a pool of shadow at the bottom of the office steps. She was tall and slim, and attractive in an unassuming way. She had long, thick hair, which was neither blond nor brown, held by clasp at the nape of her neck. She wore a simple black jacket and skirt, black shoes and hose, and a white blouse. A plain gold cross, neither small nor large, hung on a gold chain around her neck. The light shimmered on her hair and glinted on her cross, but otherwise, she seemed to draw the light in, to steal it from the very night. Of what else was she a *goniff*?

Blood.

"Don't vampires believe in knocking?" the rabbi asked.

"It's more dramatic this way."

She spoke softly, but her voice had strength to it. He imagined that she could fill the night with sound if she wanted to.

"Right now," the rabbi said, "the last thing I need in my life is more drama. Who are you?"

"Evangeline Goodwyn-Clark."

"Why are your here?"

"To make my confession," she said. "It must be the Roman Catholic in me, this need of mine to confess."

"In case you haven't noticed, I'm a Jew," he said. "We don't practice confession, not in the way you do."

"God won't mind, and you need to hear what I have to say, almost as much as I need to say it."

The rabbi tried to walk past her, but she touched his arm, stopping him. She handed him a ten-dollar bill.

"What's this?" he asked.

"I promised to repay you," she said. "The last time you saw me, I was dressed in one of my hunting outfits."

Two and two had no great way to go to make four. "You're the one who made Simeon into a vampire."

"Yes, I turned him. I suppose I went after him because I'd grown greedy and lazy and because he presented an easy target. I'd meant to take his last drop, but in the end, I couldn't bring myself to destroy him."

A wave of dizziness swept over the rabbi. "Why not?"

"Blood is a window into the soul. Would you laugh at me if I told you that Simeon was profoundly religious? He may have even been holy, even after I turned him."

A holy vampire? What kind of nonsense was that?

She continued, "At any rate, as his blood flowed into me, I came to myself. I understood that he deserved better than for me to snuff him out, and that we, all of us, needed him to exist. It was like waking from a long and fitful sleep."

The rabbi couldn't quite understand what she was telling him, if she did herself; but then again, he couldn't look into another man's blood and read the contents of his soul. "What did you do?"

"I gave him back enough of his own blood for him to stay alive. The catch is, that's how we turn people. We take their blood in and then we give a portion of it back. In the process, a portion of our own gets mixed in." The words coming in an ageless rush, she added, "It was the only way I had to keep him alive—well, undead—by that time." She remained silent for a few seconds. The light shone on her hair, and it appeared to soak into her body. "So you see, Rabbi, we're both guilty of his death in that wretched hospital room. You put him in there, but I was the one who handed you the reason to do it."

"I can't pronounce absolution, not for either one of us."

"No need. It's God who absolves, not the priest."

She came forward, moving as gracefully as though she were gliding over the paving stones instead of walking on them. She put her hands on his arms, and against his will, his body stiffened in fright.

"Don't worry. We have our rules, too, our own *mitzvot*. They place you out of bounds, not because you're unclean, but because you're the exact opposite." She touched her lips to his cheek in the profoundest of kisses. "Good night, Rabbi. *Ego te absolvo!*"

~~*

The rabbi watched her leave the courtyard, but then, rather than trudge home to his family and a micro-waved dinner, he decided to go back into the synagogue. To pray? To think? To sulk? To sit and listen to Beethoven? He had no idea.

The instant he opened the door, he caught the scent of fresh coffee. And why not? Nothing had made the slightest sense from the moment Simeon Black had first asked for his help.

The rabbi crossed the reception area and stopped outside his office. Light leaked out from under the door. No, he had not forgotten to switch it off, and besides, coffee didn't make itself. Someone was inside. He doubted it was a prowler, not in the usual sense. No, what the rabbi faced, what he could not avoid, was yet another visit from a fanger. Great. Let a legion of the undead confront him with whatever they wished. They couldn't charge him with anything of which he had not already accused himself. So be it!

With a determined push, the rabbi opened the door to his office.

Simeon Black, flushed and fit and bearing not the least resemblance to a pile of ash, stood at the coffee maker, watching the trail of brown liquid trickle into the carafe.

The rabbi gasped, but stifled it before he looked and sounded like a poorly directed reaction shot in a low-budget movie.

THE GREAT MYSTERY OF ETERNITY

Two and two may have abandoned four, but it didn't take an Einstein to figure out what had happened. One or more of the local vampires had rigged an event to trigger the hazardous-materials incident. Using the hazmat team and the confusion they'd caused as a cover, the vampires had taken Simeon off the floor, leaving behind enough of this and that to convince the authorities that he'd died in a tragic accident.

The coffeemaker sputtered.

The rabbi swung the door closed and waited a moment while his heart settled and the world resumed its normal routine: spinning about its axis, revolving about the sun, moving the seasons, day by day, one into the next.

Simeon grinned and said, "I hope you like it strong."

Giving up any residual claim he had on everyday reality, the rabbi said, "Strong is how I like to make it for myself."

"That's what I thought, but I wanted to be sure," Simeon said. "I see you've met Evangeline. Quite a girl, isn't she?" He pointed at the rabbi's face. "By the way, you have a lipstick smudge on your cheek."

"Oh, dear." The rabbi wiped it away with a paper napkin. "Thanks. My wife is a wonderful woman, but she's only so understanding."

"I know what you mean," Simeon said, and handed the rabbi a cup of coffee. "If Eva had any idea I'm here, she'd blow a gasket. I'm supposed to drop out of sight for a few years, lay low, feed out of town."

"Sounds reasonable."

Rabbi Rosenbaum needed to have one question answered before he surrendered himself to whatever awaited. "Whose ashes did your friends leave behind?"

"Oh, those," Simeon said, his voice somber. "Well. One of our rules is no clergy, no monks, no nuns, and no children. Well, that guy, the guy whose ashes you found, nailed a little boy a few weeks ago. When the community found out, they arrested him."

"Then what?"

"They disabled him in pretty much the same way you and Shapiro disabled me. Then they dressed him in my clothes, put him on my bed, filled the room with oxygen from a portable tank, opened the drapes, and let the sunrise do the rest. Before we left, they had me drain him pretty good. Between that and the occasional stray dog, I ought to be okay for a while." Simeon paused, and then added, "That guy was a real bastard, Rabbi. Pure scum." He left another silence, reflective, meditative, then he said, "We may be vampires, but we're not monsters."

Despite everything that had happened, that idea would require a little getting used to. Nevertheless, the rabbi said, "No, you're not."

The rabbi sipped his coffee. It was hot and surprisingly good, better than it often turned out when he made it.

The rabbi pulled Ima Blutsauger's book from the shelf behind his desk and handed it across to Simeon. "Here, you'll be wanting this."

"No, you'd better keep it. Once word about you spreads, you'll need a reference."

And with that bit of news, the rabbi's fragile calm shattered like the mirrored surface of a pond into which a delighted child has thrown the biggest rock he could heft.

With an effort to keep his hand from shaking, the rabbi returned the book to the shelf. Spreads. Simeon Black had said *spreads*. *Oy*! Michael Rosenbaum, rabbi to the undead.

THE GREAT MYSTERY OF ETERNITY

Cheerfully, perhaps even gleefully, Simeon added, "Don't worry. You're not alone. Fr. David Lloyd already sees a few of us, but you'll be our first rabbi in this town."

"What if I refuse?"

"You could, but you won't."

"Why not?"

"Because you're a man of deep compassion."

The rabbi shrugged. If he had that much compassion, why didn't he put these wretches out of their misery?

Because he didn't have the right to play judge, jury, and executioner, and because they weren't miserable.

Well, what about the people they killed in order to stay alive?

True, that did present a problem, one, he suspected, he'd have with him for quite a while to come. Maybe he could figure it out if he wrote a book of his own, *So Now You've Become a Chaplain to the Undead*.

Simeon topped off their coffee cups. "Rabbi," he said, "I have a problem."

"You mean in addition to finding a dentist who works at night and doesn't frighten easily?"

Simeon chuckled. "Yes, a new problem."

A sense of relief flooded through Rabbi Rosenbaum, and he smiled. Familiar words, familiar ground, at last. "What is it?"

"I've fallen in love."

"*Mazel tov!*"

"She's a few hundred years older than I am, but she loves me, and we think we can work it out. But, Rabbi, she's not Jewish."

The rabbi shook his head. This was happening so much these days. "Who's the lucky girl?" he asked. "Miss Evangeline Goodwyn-Clark?"

THE RABBI, THE VAMPIRE, AND THE MITZVOT

"Yes," Simeon said as though every endorphin in his body had rushed into his brain and exploded there. "She's a devout Roman Catholic and doesn't want to convert, and, of course, neither do I. Rabbi, can you help us?"

From the absurd to the impossible in a matter of seconds! What next?

Rabbi Rosenbaum didn't know whether to laugh, cry, or make a bad joke about finding a nice Jewish girl vampire. Instead, for the moment, as he collected his thoughts, he listened to the sounds beyond his office window.

A truck rumbled and rattled past on the street, a siren howled, a couple laughed and giggled, and no great distance away, Evangeline Goodwyn-Clark was singing the "Ode to Joy" from Beethoven's 9th. Her clear, *impossible* soprano filled the night, and Rabbi Rosenbaum realized that for as long as he lived, he would never grow weary of listening to her sing.

THE CORMORANT

An old salt and an oceanographer team up to help a cormorant with a fractured wing. They soon discover that there's something really, truly special about their patient.

MARTY EPSOM was wintering over on an inside row in the Port of Newport's South Beach Marina. The Oregon coast was a good place to hole up between the middle of October and the middle of April. The weather was never insanely cold, the marina was sheltered behind rugged rock breakwaters, there weren't many people around, and shopping was close.

He could have gone on up the Yaquina River a couple of miles and anchored out, but he'd decided that both he and his boat could use shore power and Wi-Fi. Old bones and living alone did that.

Marty got a kick out of watching the harbor seals and the sea lions: roosting on the breakwaters, chowing down on fish, shaking them apart like an excited terrier with a helpless rat in its jaws, and, now and then, hauling out on the walks and making bellowing nuisances out of themselves. When it came to hauling out, the navigation buoys were also a pinniped favorite.

The seagulls were a kick, too, when they weren't crapping on Marty's boat, an aging Pacific Seacraft 37'. Marty liked to feed them, and he liked to watch them when they'd gotten into the Rogue Brewery's discarded mash. Then they ended up staggering drunk and littering the walkways with their mash-laden vomit and poop. It looked like piles of soggy sawdust or miniprestologs that had been left out in the rain. It didn't really give off much of an odor.

Marty's enjoyment wasn't a case of schadenfreude, but of fellow feeling. Been there, done that. Just be glad you don't have to roll out at oh-dark-thirty. Maybe they did, though. Poor bastards.

Gluttonous seagulls.

It made sense, but who'd a-thunk it?

When Marty was bored, one of the ways he amused himself was to hose the gull-processed brewery mash, for lack of a better term, off the walkways.

Marty was easily amused, as he would be the first to admit.

Newport: a comfortable place.

As Christmas faded into history and January settled in for a nice chatty, halyard-banging visit, what began to puzzle Marty about the local fauna was the number of cormorants around.

Their locations and numbers varied, often wildly, up and down the bay, up and down the coast. Like the sea lions.

But that was the whole point.

The cormorant's numbers seemed to have stabilized and then grown. They were taking over the marina, and they lined the crabbing pier's railings as well. The birds looked like so many black, avian uprights. The spaces between them reminded Marty of medieval crenellations.

It wasn't just the marina and the crabbing pier. Everywhere Marty looked he saw cormorants roosting, their wings spread to dry, their heads swiveling this way and that, taking in their surroundings, always on watch, always on the lookout. Their beaks were long and sharp and viciously hooked, like the barbs on a fishing spear.

The whole thing was perfectly normal, but it was also perfectly creepy. They ought to have moved on. Their numbers ought to be fluctuating. Their vigilance ought to slack off, no matter how briefly, but it never did.

And, too, they looked larger, sleeker, and more powerful than the cormorants Marty was used to seeing on his travels. Their feathers were a deeper shade of black, if that were possible—a black that verged on the iridescent.

The cormorants weren't hurting anything, except to clobber the bay's stock of fish, but once the birds had moved on, the fish would bounce back. If the fish could survive the seals and the sea lions and the sports fishermen, they ought to be able to survive a few birds. Individual fish, not so much, but the schools would be okay.

So Marty set his concerns aside and occupied himself with reading, working on his boat, *Geezer's Revenge*, snagging lunch now and then at the brewery, and going for long walks, rain or shine.

The Oregon Coast Aquarium and the Hatfield Marine Science Center were two favorites for easy strolls when he needed to work off a little restlessness as opposed to a serious hike to work out the kinks and keep the blood pumping, the muscles from going winter-soft.

One morning he was leaving for a hike, not a stroll, weights in hand, when he found a dazed cormorant huddling on the sole of *Geezer*'s cockpit. One of the bird's wings was bent at an angle that couldn't be healthy. The bird must have broken it.

Marty tried to imagine what had happened.

The best he could come up with was that a freak gust of wind had smacked the bird into *Geezer*'s rigging, or maybe into her mast or her boom.

THE GREAT MYSTERY OF ETERNITY

The more Marty looked at the cormorant, the less and less dazed it became. It flopped back and forth, giving every indication of trying to escape, but, naturally, with its broken wing, it couldn't.

As Marty had figured, the bird was larger than average, the beak a touch longer, and the hook a bit sharper looking. The bird's eyes, which were as black as its feathers, were bright but not with panic. Rather, Marty would have guessed that the bird was disgusted with itself for having broken its wing.

Marty could relate, as multiple scars could attest: a childhood broken arm and multiple fishhook punctures, among others.

Ten, or perhaps fifteen, cormorants circled the boat, flying a couple of yards above mast height, call it sixty feet or so off the water. Now and then, they appeared to Marty as though they were staring down critically into the cockpit of his boat.

One landed on the bow pulpit, then another landed on the starboard spreader, and finally one landed on a lifeline, close to the portside cap shroud. They looked at him with an unsettling combination of worry, hope, and hostility.

Well, let 'em look.

If they decided to come after him, then all bets were off, but in the meantime, if they left him alone, he'd leave them alone.

Howsomever, Marty couldn't leave the injured cormorant in his boat's cockpit to die, he couldn't toss it overboard for the same reason, and he wasn't about to wring its neck. As long as it was alive, there ought to be something that could be done for it.

If a killer whale had eaten it, Marty wouldn't have batted an eye, but this ... this was different.

Therefore, after much deliberation and against his saner

judgement with respect to tactics, Marty put on a pair of leather cloves, the fur-lined ones he wore when the weather turned really cold, and cornered the now frantic, squawking bird.

Marty talked to it. "You're hurt, but I think I know somebody who might be able to help. You'll be fine. You're as good as dead if I don't do something, and you may end up dead even if I do, but this way at least you've got a chance." He tried to think of what else he could say, but he couldn't.

The circling birds circled closer. The perched, watching birds watched more intently, their heads barely moving.

It took several attempts, but in the end, Marty managed to pick up the injured cormorant. Significantly, he performed this feat without the bird ripping out Marty's eyes or opening the side of his face. One of his gloves would never be the same, and there was now a three-corner tear, more of a cut, really, in his jacket sleeve.

The bird was heavier than Marty had expected, the feathers smoother, slicker than he would have anticipated. Then again, he didn't spend a lot of time messing around with cormorants, so what the hell did he know.

The circling birds did not attack. The watching birds continued their vigil. But they seemed to be doing so with greater intent. If they'd been locked and loaded before, they were now only loaded—safeties off.

Seen up close the cormorant's bill was a weapon to behold. And why not? Cormorants were accomplished hunters, both as individuals and in flocks.

"Easy, easy," Marty said, as soothingly as he could. "Calm down and we'll both be all right."

He held the struggling bird against his jacket, a bit like a football, careful not to put any pressure on the broken wing.

"How's that?"

The bird was bulkier, too, and it didn't give off much of an odor.

Oddly, once the bird was cradled, it quit squawking and settled. It lay quietly. It was very un-birdlike behavior.

For a second there, Marty was afraid that it might have died or passed out, but no, it was moving its head, looking around.

"Okay, pal," Marty said, "Here we go."

No response from the bird.

Marty gingerly stepped from *Geezer*'s deck across to the finger walk. From there, he figured it would be duck soup to take the bird up to the Marine Science Center.

~~*

By the time Marty had walked as far as the ramp up to the parking lot, he regretted his choice of words. Cormorants lined the ridge line of the utility building, where the heads were, they lined the railing that did what it could to discourage people from stumbling over the bank and tumbling down the riprap and into the water, and they were wheeling in a tight circle above his head. Every one of them was glaring at him as though they'd like nothing better than to rip his throat out.

Duck soup. Had they read his mind? Hadn't they ever heard of the Marx Brothers?

Marty brought his thoughts to heel.

No, they'd never heard of the Marx Brothers. They were wild birds and had probably never seen a television set, let alone gone to a Marx-Brothers revival.

No, they hadn't read his mind. Mind reading was the stuff of fiction.

Yes, they were likely keeping an eye on both him and the cormorant he was carrying. This was something of a stretch, but it was the only thing that came anywhere close to explaining their behavior and their attitude of silent, potential menace—safeties off, rounds chambered, but fingers on trigger guards.

~~*

It took some doing, but a few minutes later, Marty was standing in the Center's lobby, talking to Dr. Amanda Gold, a vet who'd switched to marine biology. She was in her early forties, neither thin nor heavy, a hiker rather than a runner. Living up to her last name, she had blond hair, which was beginning to gray.

Gold wasn't exactly a friend, but she wasn't exactly a stranger. He'd first met her a few weeks ago down on one of the marina's docks. She'd been using a net to coax a very large, yellow jellyfish into a blue-plastic bucket. It was wet, cold work, and he'd offered to help, either by holding the bucket or by working the net. She'd asked him to hold the bucket.

The lobby was cool and smelled of "marine life," fish, shellfish, and God only knew what else. The atmosphere damp. The floors were polished concrete, the accents varnished fir, and the lighting florescent where it wasn't LED bulbs.

Gesturing at the bird, Gold asked, "Who's your friend?"

"Found it on my boat," Marty said. "Can you do anything for it?"

She looked.

"Broken wing," she said.

THE GREAT MYSTERY OF ETERNITY

Duh.

"Which means?" he asked.

"Broken wings are hard. Bird bones are light and brittle. They're hard to set, and they don't always heal as well as one would like, if they heal at all." She stroked the top of the bird's head.

Marty noticed that the cormorant didn't try rip a three-corner tear in Gold's sleeve, or in the back of her hand, or anywhere else. How'd she rate? Still, smart bird. Make friends while the making's good.

"More often than not," Gold said, "the kindest thing to do is to euthanize."

"Crap," Marty said.

"I can do it, if you'd like."

"No, I wouldn't like."

"Do you want to do it?"

"No, I want you to set its wing."

Out of the corner of his eye, Marty caught a glimpse of the receptionist rolling her eyes.

Marty added, "I can pay for it."

"Never mind about that," Amanda said. "The trick is going to be figuring out how to set and splint the break." She frowned. "Every case is unique."

They took the cormorant into a lab that doubled as a veterinary exam and treatment room. The walls, ceiling, and floors were white. The fixtures were stainless steel and green Formica. The air smelled of bleach and rubbing alcohol.

It reminded Marty of places he would rather forget but never would.

They put the bird on the examination table. Dr. Gold slipped on a pair of exam gloves and got to work. She murmured to the bird, as humans do, as though they expected the bird to understand.

Gold hadn't gotten far when her face paled, and she froze in place. She looked like a "living statue" in a veterinary diorama on career day. After a couple of seconds, she "came back to life," pursed her lips, shook her head. The light flashed off her hair, and Marty caught a flash of the lilac scent of the shampoo she'd used that morning.

"Come over here and take a look at this," she said, and slightly repositioned the bird's wing.

Marty went around and looked down, expecting the worse, a verdict that nothing could be done.

"What am I looking at?" Marty asked.

Gold smiled at him, or tried to. "Never took biology?"

"Nope."

"First aid?"

"Some." He did not tell her that he'd majored in bullet dodging at LBJ University's Kennedy School of Southeast Asian Affairs.

"It's a compound fracture. The radius has snapped, and one end of it is protruding through the skin."

He looked again. "Okay, I can see what you're talking about, but you can set it, right?"

She arched an eyebrow. "Take a closer gander at that bone."

He did, and felt his stomach hollow out. His mouth wet dry and the muscles up the back of his neck went rigid. "That's not bone."

"Not hardly," she said.

"So what is it?"

"Plastic, at a guess," she said. "The question is, what's a living, breathing cormorant doing with an artificial radius?"

It was a good question, but Marty didn't have the ghost of an answer, so he kept his mouth shut.

Gold went to work: bone sample, blood sample, and a bunch of tests Marty could only guess at. First aid classes—the treatment of sucking chest wounds had been a special favorite—and a lifetime spent avoiding doctors whenever possible had left Marty's medical knowledge a little on the sketchy side.

A full-body X-ray of the bird would have been nice, but they couldn't figure out how to take one, not with the equipment available, not without exposing themselves to the X-rays while simultaneously doing their best to hold the bird in place.

Nevertheless, Gold had a battery of tests she could perform, and she moved from one to another with an outward surety and calm that her edgy tone of voice and trembling hands put the lie to.

Meanwhile, the bird squawked and shuffled around from time to time, but all in all, it didn't put up much of a fuss.

Eventually, they parked the bird in a cage and waited for the various analyzers to finish analyzing.

Gold looked at the bone sample through a microscope.

"I was right," she said. "It's some kind of composite. Definitely not bone—not bone bone if you take my meaning."

Marty did. "Peachy," he said.

"*Peachy*? I'd have expected stronger from an old salt like you."

"I promised my mother."

She chuckled at the lame joke.

"We've got a few minutes," she said. "Coffee?"

"Is it hot and wet?"

THE CORMORANT

"Most of the time."
"Lead on, Macduff."

~~*

The Center's breakroom was a cross between a low-budget Starbucks and a micro-cafeteria. A guy with dreadlocks and a Bob Marley T-shirt ran the espresso machine. Three vending machines sat in a row along one wall, and a couple of cafeteria tables with plastic chairs held sway in the center of the room.

The brewed coffee was in two thermoses on the counter: regular and decaf.

Gold and the barista bantered back and forth, and Gold drew a cup of brewed regular. Marty followed suit. They paid for their coffees, both black, and sat at the far end of the room, by the floor-to-ceiling windows. The cold from outside cascaded down from the glass and puddled on the floor, chilling Marty's feet.

Gold said, "I'll have to use epoxy and hope it holds. I don't dare try anything else."

"Model-airplane glue?"

She shook her head. "No, that works by melting one piece into the other."

This was a fact that a much younger Marty had learned to his cost and the ruination of a B-17, a P-51, and a Sherman Tank. He'd finally read *all* of the instructions, wrapped his head around them, and the ME 109 had turned out well enough—before he'd painted it. The Israelis had flown 109s in the '48 war, having ferried them in from Czechoslovakia, so Marty painted his model in what he'd figured had to have been the Israeli colors. Unfortunately, there was more to painting a model airplane than slapping on the paint. Keeping it off his hands, desk, and clothes, for example. And out of his hair.

Gold said, "Without knowing the exact chemical composition of the radius, I don't dare. I could wind up dissolving the whole thing."

"Not good."

"No, especially for the bird ... or whatever it is."

~~*

Whatever it was, it wasn't a bird.

The analyses showed that the blood wasn't blood. It was a red fluid, all right, but it was not blood. The microscope revealed cells in a multitude of shapes and sizes, but they were unlike anything Gold had ever seen before.

The genetic tests came up blank. The samples ought to have been crawling with DNA, but the analyzer couldn't detect any, nothing that it recognized as DNA. Of course, there was nothing that said it had to.

The bird stood on the examination table. It held its broken wing away from its body, but otherwise looked from Gold to Marty and back again. With every passing minute, it was behaving less and less like a bird.

"Is it biological or is it a machine?" Marty said. Racing ahead he added, "I don't see how a living thing could grow composite bones."

"Why not?" Gold said. "A lot of people would argue that we are nothing but meat machines."

"You really know how to buck up a guy's self-esteem, don't you?"

"I'm not in the self-esteem business, I'm in the science business," she said, not unkindly.

Marty asked, "What now, kemosabe?"

"I treat the patient."

"Then what?"

"Then we make up our minds about the next step."

Gold washed the wound and sterilized the area around it. The break wasn't clean, like a snapped pencil, but looked more like a green twig that had split along the grain. That a composite would behave like that was another question that couldn't be answered, not immediately, if ever.

"I can't inject the area around the bone with an analgesic," Gold said. "God only knows what it would do to the bird. I guess the bird and I have no choice but to gut it out."

"Maybe not," Marty said, and hurried out.

He went to the breakroom, begged a large cup of ice from the Bob Marley wannabe, and rushed back to the lab.

Marty handed the cup to Gold. "Try this," he said. He did not tell her about his pierced ear, long since abandoned and grown closed.

"Ice," she said. "Of course. I should have thought of that. Assuming that cold will deaden this critter's pain sensors."

"It might not work, but it won't do any harm."

"That we know of."

Marty shrugged. "So sue me," he said good naturedly. He did not tell her about the decades of his life he had lost to overthinking and the pursuit of perfection—the perfect wife, the perfect religion, the perfect career, the perfect boat.

"You're absolutely right, though," Gold said, and spilled a few cubes of ice into her hand.

THE GREAT MYSTERY OF ETERNITY

She applied them to the break and waited.

The bird as good as tapped a foot, also waiting.

After a couple of minutes, Gold said, "That ought to do it."

Meanwhile, Marty had been mixing up about a tablespoon's worth of medical-grade, fast-setting epoxy. Giving it a final stir, he said, "It's ready."

Gold carefully coated the bone splinters, pressed them together, bound them with a fine, inert thread, and coated the outside of the break.

The bird put up a fuss, but that was understandable. Ice or no ice, the procedure must had caused it no small amount of "discomfort." A 7.62X54R slug from a Viet Cong Mosin-Nagant M44 rifle, Russian supplied, had taught Marty everything he'd ever needed to know and then some about "discomfort." And the parts the M44 had overlooked, various fishing hooks, hammers, and back spasms had supplied later on.

Once the epoxy had gone off, Gold again disinfected the area and closed it with ordinary dissolving sutures. With that step out of the way, she applied a liquid bandage. The final step was to splint the break and immobilize it by taping the wing to the bird's body.

By the time she stood away, the bird was breathing heavily and, if Marty hadn't known any better, was looking a trifle pale.

They put the bird back in the cage, provided it food and water, and left it to rest.

~~*

From the Marine Science Center Marty and Gold walked over toward the NOAA docks. The wind gusted across the bay,

THE CORMORANT

raw and cold, snapping the flags and kicking up a low chop. The asphalt was grainy underfoot. It felt like walking on sandpaper or on a deck that's been painted with aggressive nonskid.

Marty imagined he could still smell the lab, still taste it in his mouth, smell it clinging to his clothes. He'd always hated that smell. Physics labs were okay, but biology labs were too, well, organic for his taste. They reminded him of med stations and ambulances, of hospitals and doctors' offices.

And yet the Marine Science Center was one of his favorite places. Go figure.

A plume of gray-black smoke was rising from the stack of one of the NOAA ships. As ships went, the NOAA vessels weren't very large, but they were bigger than most of the buildings along Newport's bay front, over on the north side of the water.

"The cormorant ought to recover, oughtn't it?" Marty said. Without using his fingers he'd put air-quotes around the word *cormorant*.

"I hope," Gold said. "We'll know one way or the other in a couple of days. There are more ifs than I care to count."

They walked on silently, side by side.

Dogs are said to be able to tell when someone is staring at them. However that felt to a dog, Marty was having what he could only think of as a very similar feeling, tickling up and down the back of his neck, tightening the muscles along his cervical spine.

It was the same sort of feeling he'd gotten on the Duck Quick campus of LBJU, right before the Viet Cong sniper rounds started to streak in, taking off heads, opening chests, and rearranging intestines.

It was thanks to that feeling, that sense of being watched, that he had developed a knack for moving out of the line of fire before the firing started, a knack that had allowed him to graduate, when so many of his buddies hadn't.

He could think of only one time that his knack had failed him, a couple of weeks before he'd been scheduled to go home, a notoriously dangerous time, a time when his head hadn't been entirely in the game.

The wind coming across the bay gusted, whipping his pants legs.

Despite the wind, the sense of being watched deepened. Therefore, acting on this here-and-now replay of that old, reliable sensation, Marty stopped and looked back along the way he and Amanda Gold had come.

Stopping was a bad idea, but he figured it might throw them off, show them that he wasn't afraid.

Good luck on that score.

Glowering cormorants lined the roof of the Marine Science Center, and several more of them were circling directly overhead. They gave every evidence of not giving a rat's ass whether Marty was afraid of them or not. The eyes of a brave man will come out just as easily as the eyes of a coward.

Well? Would there be incoming or not?

With seagulls it would have been a sure thing, but with cormorants the situation wasn't as easy to read. For one thing, as far as Marty could tell, cormorants were way, way smarter than seagulls.

Cormorants. If that's what these birds were.

Thanks to JFK, the CIA, and LBJ, Marty had learned that it *was* in fact possible to squeeze his entire body into his helmet. The laws of physics might have maintained differently, but

Marty was living proof that it could be done.

His only regret at the moment was that he didn't have a helmet to climb into.

Without looking back, Gold said, "We're being watched?"

"That we are," Marty said.

They resumed walking.

Marty said, "That cormorant's body was designed, produced, and then populated with an intelligence."

"No argument from me."

"Its buddies, too."

"And your point is?"

"So what are they and who sent them?" Marty asked.

Gold shrugged, made a dismissive gesture. "They're the advance cohorts of the space army of the Emperor Ming the Merciless, all the way from the planet Mongo."

"Well, that clears that up, Dr. Zarkova."

"Happy to be of help, Flash."

"Okay," Marty said. "How about this one, then: they could have picked any form they'd wanted."

"Sounds reasonable. What's your point?"

"Why'd they choose cormorants?"

Gold shrugged. "Maybe they like raw fish."

"Works for me," Marty said.

They walked on for a time. Marty thought he caught a whiff of creosote. A gull swooped in low, crying, and amid a flapping of wings, which made a low-pitched, dull, squeaking sound, forced another gull off the top of a piling.

Marty asked, "Well, what do you want to do?"

"As soon as its ready, we'll release it back into the wild."

"Shouldn't we report it?"

"Is that what you want to do?"

"No. I believe in live and let live, as long as it's mutual," Marty said.

"Me, too," she said. "The minute we told anyone about cormorants from another world, my career would be over and they'd accuse you of having watched one too many Alfred Hitchcock movies. They'd back ball me, and lock you up in a padded cell." Her voice steely, she added, "They'd dissect the bird."

"Ming the Merciless wouldn't like that much, would he?"

"No, he would not," she said. "Besides, I don't look good in tinfoil. Very unflattering."

Another dozen paces.

A cold suggestion of rain, the first prickling drops stippling the ground, their jackets.

Marty said, "You forgot the part where they charge us with animal cruelty."

"You must have worked for the government," she said.

"In another life," Marty said. He did not tell her about draft boards, the Gulf of Tonkin Resolution, and "light at the end of the tunnel."

~~*

Five days later, Gold called Marty. The epoxy had cured, as opposed to merely having set; the wing was healing nicely; and the bird was eating like a horse. It was rested and restless.

"Sounds like it's time to turn it loose," Marty said.

"Wanna be here?"

"I'll come right over."

THE CORMORANT

~~*

Marty and Gold loaded the bird's cage onto a cart and wheeled it out into a parking lot.

The weather had changed from low, rain-heavy clouds and blustering winds to bright winter sunshine and a dead calm. Without falling into a state of complete delusion, Marty could imagine that the crocuses were about to pop up and that the Scotch broom was on the verge of blooming, that spring had come early.

It hadn't, and Marty knew it.

Still, it was a beautiful day. Good for a row, good for a long hike, good for a walk on the beach, maybe pick up an agate or two. Stop and smell the sand, the surf, the weed exposed at low tide.

Cormorants lined the edge of the roof and a nearby fence.

At Gold's invitation, Marty opened the cage.

The bird stepped out—no frantic rush to escape—spread its wings as though drying them, and gave them a tentative flap. Apparently satisfied with the result, it leaped into the air.

It gained altitude and circled back over the Marine Science Center. As it did, the waiting, watching cormorants, or whatever they actually were, took off in a body and joined it. As a flock, they wheel and headed toward the South Beach Marina, toward the breakwater where they'd been roosting.

~~*

Two days later, or maybe it was three, a decidedly avian commotion close aboard *Geezer's Revenge* roused Marty from a sound sleep.

The weather had turned cold, and his electric heater was thrumming away. Electric heat on a small boat was one of the coveted luxuries of being alongside. Anchoring out was cheaper, but anchoring out meant no shore power.

A heavy thump came from the cockpit, followed by frenetic, lesser thumps.

Marty cut loose with a string of muttered, salty invectives, and curled off the settee. He usually slept on the settee, preferring it to the V-berth in the forepeak. For one thing, the V-berth had a closed-in feeling that he didn't like, especially now that he was getting genuinely older, and for another, from the settee it was easy for him to get up on deck in a hurry, especially when he was at sea.

Marty pulled on a pair pants, the ones he'd be wearing the day before, for several days before, and a jacket that was decorated with daubs of paint, drips of epoxy, and several unidentifiable brown-black splotches. They were grease and oil mostly but not exclusively. He pulled a dark-blue watch cap down onto his head and opened the companionway hatch.

The clouds were back, low and gray, and the wind had picked up, but not much. Here and there, halyards were slapping lazily against masts. The air smelled like rain. Or, perish the thought, perhaps like snow. At the coast? Now and then. Why not? Snow on the beach. A treat for the locals.

Judging by where the walkways were riding against the pilings, it was a little after high tide. Even without a handy-dandy piling, Marty fancied that he could tell what the tide was doing. He liked to think he could feel it through the bottoms of his feet, like the depth of the water, regardless of the tide, or the speed of the current and the set of the eddies through a narrow pass.

Like as not, it was romantic bullshit, but Marty delighted in indulging himself in it.

Cormorants lined the boat's stern pulpit. To Marty, they all looked pretty much alike, some a trifle larger, some a trifle smaller, but one was holding a wing slightly away from its body.

"Well, hello there," Marty said. "How're you doing?"

A polite squawking in reply.

More of the thumping interrupted.

It was coming from a salmon, thrashing in the well of the cockpit.

Marty looked from the fish to the birds, from the birds to the fish, and back to the birds.

"Thank you," Marty said.

The birds squawked for a moment or two and then took off.

By the middle of the day they had left the bay, and Marty was once again alone with his boat, *Geezer's Revenge*.

THREE GUYS AND A BAR

This story features the series characters the Old Man, the Kid, and the Swami. They build things and solve problems. They love their projects and stand ready to help in times of need.

When the occupants of one of their creations ask for their help, they sail to the rescue. Sadly, it isn't long before the three guys find themselves up against a deadly enemy.

SO THESE THREE GUYS eased their cruising-style sailboat in toward a guest dock that might have been in a bay on the Sunshine Coast of British Columbia. If the light had been better, and not a persistent, pea-soup fog, the place would have looked like Gibson's Landing, or Secret Cove, or Pender Harbour. Or maybe Egmont. Nice places. All different, but all the same: docks on the water and one or more bars up on the shore. Fir trees and rocks. Harbor seals and cormorants. Seagulls and beer.

Small craft filled the moorage: runabouts, cabin cruisers, fish boats, and sailboats. Several of them rafted.

A pole lamp stood guard at the outboard end of the guest dock. The dock was deserted.

"They asked for our help, didn't they?" the kid said.

"They did."

"And they knew we were coming, didn't they?"

"They did," the old man said.

"Well, then, where are they?" the kid asked.

"Good question," the old man said.

"Fear can be doing regrettable things to people," the swami said.

THE GREAT MYSTERY OF ETERNITY

"Tell me about it," the kid said.

A ramp connected the moorage to a bar up on the shore. The bar was larger than most. It was a lodge-style building with a high, peaked roof, huge windows, and lots of stonework. A flashing neon sign sat perched along the roofline.

The kid felt a pang of recognition, a jolt of builder's remorse. He had done the best he could. He had held nothing back. And yet the place, beguiled, had veered into a first-class mess.

The kitchen's exhaust fan made a dull, rhythmic squeak, as though it couldn't make up its mind whether to go on working or not.

The air smelled, to one of the guys, like fir trees, maple trees, and rhododendron bushes; to another, it smelled like wet sand—shingle, to be precise—and seaweed; and to the last guy, it smelled like their boat's diesel exhaust and the bar's overcooked food.

Their boat was a heavy-displacement ketch, forty-some feet long, thirty-some years old. She was fresh out of her annual yard period and smelled like paint, varnish, wax, metal polish, and sealant. Even in this dull light her brightwork sparkled. Her sails were neatly stowed under their shiny blue covers.

Less than a dozen yards from the dock, the old man, the one who smelled fir trees, gave the engine a shot of reverse, and the boat slowed from a walk to a crawl.

A lazy swell drifted into the bay from the strait outside, and a whisper of wind ghosted across the boat's starboard quarter. Together, the swell and the wind gently pushed the boat toward the guest dock.

The old man eased the wheel over, and the boat pointed more sharply toward the dock.

THREE GUYS AND A BAR

Idling, the engine made a low rumble. The spent water from the heat exchanger splashed into the bay.

The kid, the one who'd smelled wet shingle and seaweed, stepped across onto the dock and hitched a spring line around the bullrail. He jogged aft toward the boat's stern, not hurrying.

The old man spun the wheel, and the boat's stern tucked in as pretty as could be.

Before the kid arrived, the swami, the one who'd smelled diesel exhaust and overcooked food, tossed the loose end of the stern line across in a lazy arc.

Instantly, the swami was also on the dock. He was in two places at the same time. The swami on the dock caught the line the swami on the boat had just thrown. The swami on the dock tied off the line.

"Now cut that out," the kid groused.

"I am so very sorry," the swami on the dock said. "I was only making an effort to be of help."

The kid shook his head. "Well, don't. It's unnerving," he said. "How do you do that, anyway?"

The swami on the boat pressed his hands together over his heart, bowed, and vanished.

The swami on the dock said, "I am most assuredly a swami, am I not? It is in my nature to do such things."

"Yeah, but *how*?"

"As I have tried so very many times to explain it to you," the swami said, not unkindly, "all of space and all of time are united in a single, eternal unity. All time is *now*. All places are *here*. Moreover, *now* and *here* are the same thing." He smiled. "In fact, *thing*-ness itself is an illusion. It is most assuredly the desperate creation of our—"

THE GREAT MYSTERY OF ETERNITY

"All right, knock it off you two," the old man said. "Secure the bow line."

The kid ran forward.

A second swami appeared on the bow and tossed the line across.

The kid grimaced in exasperation, but without a word, he tied off the bow line.

"Okay," he called aft, and nodded his thanks to the swami, who smiled in return.

"We're here," the old man announced, and killed the engine.

The swami on the bow disappeared.

The day's fog-wrapped silence pounced on them like a ravenous mountain cat.

Trapped between the boat and the dock, the fenders made an ugly, rustling noise. It sounded like dry fingers being drawn across a party balloon.

The old man stepped down onto the dock.

"Something's wrong," he said. He pointed up toward the shore. "There ought to be music coming from the bar, but there isn't. Not a peep."

"Maybe they're closed," the kid said.

"Then why is the sign lit up?" the old man said.

"I genuinely do not mean to change the subject, but where are we?" the swami asked.

"I thought we were *everywhere*," the kid said.

"That is most assuredly true," the swami said. "However, I was wondering where this most unique *everywhere* happens to *be*."

"Still disoriented from the crossing?" the old man asked.

"Yes, a tad," the swami said.

THREE GUYS AND A BAR

"We all are," the old man said.

"Crossings will do that," the kid said.

He sighed. "Don't either of you recognize it?"

"Should we?" the old man asked. "I just followed the waypoints."

"Yes, you ought to," the kid said. "We built it."

The swami's face lit up. "Oh, yes. So we did."

"That was a long time ago," the old man said.

"Ages," the swami said.

The red-blue light of the neon sign pounded through the fog.

The old man shook his head. "They've made a lot of changes. That hideous sign for one."

"Too many changes," the swami said.

"Time flies," the kid said.

A man stepped out of the shadows at the base of the ramp that led up to the bar. He was dressed in brown hiking boots, blue denim pants, a navy-blue flannel shirt, a red-and-black plaid lumberman's jacket, and a tan canvas hat, the kind with a downturned brim. He was tall and looked thinner than might be healthy.

"Who are you?" the old man asked.

"I'm the publican," the man from the shadows said. "How was your crossing?"

"Fine," the old man said.

"Did you manage to do any sailing on your way across?"

"No, but maybe on the way back," the old man said.

The swami said, "Sailing is great fun, most rewarding."

"How about the waypoints I sent you?" the publican asked. "Were they adequate? The entrance has changed over the years, and there've been one or two wrecks."

THE GREAT MYSTERY OF ETERNITY

"We made it," the old man said.

"So you did," the publican said. "I'm kind of surprised you came, after all this time and everything."

"Forget about *everything*. Why did you send for us?" the old man asked.

"And why weren't you there to at least catch our lines?" the kid asked, and immediately regretted the harshness that had crept into his voice.

"I have to be cautious these days."

"Perhaps more caution yesterday would have allowed you less caution today," the swami said.

"True. Very true." the publican said. He pointed toward the bar, toward the roof. "Did you notice our new sign?"

The three guys looked up at the sign again. This time they studied it more carefully, as though they had never seen it before.

It overlooked the water like a garish beacon and spelled out

THE EARTH

in red, white, and blue neon letters a meter tall.

"We saw it on the way in," the old man said.

"What do you think of it?" the publican asked.

"I think it's a lot of sign," the old man said.

"Why neon?" the kid asked.

"It brings in the business," the publican said.

The old man cocked an eyebrow. "And what else?"

"Complaints."

"It was ever thus," the swami said. "The instant one man figures out a way to make a better living than his fellows, another man most assuredly figures out a way to thwart him. It is indeed very sad. Most lamentable. Rather than build up, people seem determined to tear down."

"That's envy for you," the kid commented. "It always leads to trouble."

To the publican, the old man said, "Complaints and ...?"

"That sign is the reason I asked you to come," the publican said. "That's where it all started."

"Where all *what* started?" the old man asked.

"It seems we're in violation of a dozen different building and zoning codes."

The old man arched an eyebrow. "Whose codes?" he asked.

"Ours. At least, we agreed to them. You know how it is."

"Peachy," the old man said sardonically.

"That was my reaction, once we'd figured out what we'd done," the publican said.

"What about your homes and farms?" the old man asked.

"The codes don't cover them, only the bar."

"Well, that's something," the old man said.

"Let's go on up," the publican said. "Everyone's waiting for you."

The publican started toward the bottom of the ramp, but the old man held back.

"This is your mess," the old man said. "Maybe you ought to be the ones to sort it out."

"You really don't want to leave them hanging, do you?" the kid asked the old man.

The old man glared at him for a long moment. Then he sighed, as though shifting from one conclusion to another much less attractive one. "No, not really. Although it is tempting."

THE GREAT MYSTERY OF ETERNITY

~~*

From the outside, and closer to, the bar looked like a cross between a Swiss chalet and a Tudor tavern. Like the neon sign up on the roof, the signboard over the front door announced that the establishment was The Earth and showed the blue-and-white marble of NASA fame. Cars, pickup trucks, and motorcycles crowded the parking lot. Bicycles leaned against various lamp and barrier posts.

Parked in a place apart, bathed in the light of a mercury-vapor lamp, sat a low-slung, high-end, flame-red sports car. It was not a sports sedan, nor a sport utility vehicle, nor an outsized convertible, but a genuine two-seater, go-really-really-fast sports car.

"*He*'s here," the old man said.

"Where else would you expect him to be?" the swami said.

"I plan on ignoring him as long as possible," the kid said.

"Good plan, but it never works," the old man said. "Pretending he doesn't exist only encourages him."

"I have no intention of *pretending* he doesn't exist," the kid said. "I only intend to ignore his blandishments."

"Much nearer to the point," the swami said, "what is he doing *here*?"

"Making a nuisance of himself, of course," the old man said.

"Nuisance isn't the half of it," the publican said.

"I didn't think so," the old man said.

"There are days when I wish I'd stuck to tax collecting," the publican said, and led them inside.

~~*

THREE GUYS AND A BAR

From the inside, the bar looked exactly as though it belonged to the outside. The place was part ski resort, part hunting lodge, part sports bar, part pub, and, oddly enough—or perhaps appropriately enough—part courtroom. That added up to a lot of parts, but somehow The Earth carried it off.

The air had a cold, damp feel to it, despite a fireplace with a wood fire, despite the press of people. The place smelled of beer, popcorn, fried food, peanuts, wood polish, and frightened humanity.

The people gave them a round of applause and shouts of welcome, but the publican waved the patrons to silence.

"Time enough for that later," he said. "Right now, they've had a tricky crossing, what with the fog and all, and need to get a little something warm inside them."

The publican guided them to a table, and within seconds, a blushing waitress came over.

The publican ordered a round of beers and burger baskets.

"The beer's excellent," he said. "The burgers are so-so."

"So-so is good," the old man said.

The beers arrived first.

The old man, the kid, and the Swami sipped at their glasses and said how much they liked it.

The old man said, "Tell us again. Exactly what are you asking us to do?"

Before the publican could answer, the kid said, "I don't feel so good."

"What's wrong?" the old man asked. "Did the beer make you sick?"

"No, it's not that. It's just that I feel as though there are two of me. You know, like there's a me and another me trapped inside the same *me*. It's really strange."

The swami said, "Now that you are mentioning it, I feel it, too. It is indeed most unsettling."

The old man thought a moment, and then said, "Count me in." He sipped his beer. He made a face and set it aside. He signaled to the waitress.

She hurried over, too anxious.

The old man ordered a cup of coffee. Fresh if they had it. If not, he'd pay them to make a fresh pot.

She gushed about how that wouldn't be necessary. They'd gladly make a fresh pot. She sped away.

"This happens every time we build something," the kid said. "Every time we go anywhere near anything we've ever built .... Every stinking time."

"I know," the old man said. "And we all feel it, thanks to you." He turned to the publican. "You still haven't answered my question. What do you expect us to do that you can't already do for yourselves?"

"Let's eat first," the publican said.

"That bad, eh?"

"Might be."

For the next few minutes, they chatted about making the crossing in the fog, about the way the entrance to the bay had changed over the years, about the wrecks the publican had mentioned, about the weird sounds killer whales made when they breathed.

The coffee arrived. It was fresh, hot, and strong enough to float an egg.

They chatted about floods, and desert hikes, and the dietary habits of whales.

THREE GUYS AND A BAR

Their burgers arrived. They were better than so-so, especially after several hours on the water in a cold, penetrating fog.

They ate and talked about politics and about the perils of building anything. No matter what it was—hovel, palace, temple, or cathedral—there were always risks. There were always uncertainties. There was always the fear of shoddy workmanship. And in the end, there was always the fear that the project could have turned out better than it had.

When they'd finished eating, when the old man had drunk two more cups of coffee, he said to the publican, "It's time for you to quit stalling. Tell us about the code violations."

"What it amounts to is this, the place needed a facelift," the publican said. "We got started okay, but then, well, things sort of went pair-shaped," the publican said. "Who better to set things to rights than the guys who built it in the first place?"

The old man pointedly swept his gaze around the room. "And all these people are here just to watch us do our thing?"

In ones, twos, and threes, the people in the room glanced up from their drinks and turned their attention toward the three guys and the publican.

The publican said, "They're The Earth's loyal patrons."

"Something most assuredly does not smell right," the swami said.

"I agree," the kid said. "What's really going on? *He* isn't here by accident."

"It *is* a repair job," the publican said. "Essentially."

By this time, all conversation in the room had ground to a halt and every eye in the place was trained toward them.

Even the cook had come out from the back. He stood leaning against the kitchen door, his arms crossed over his chest.

He glared at them as he might glare at a bulging can of stewed tomatoes.

Just then, a man stood up in a far corner of the room. Most of the people in the bar were dressed in casual clothes, but not him. He had on gray slacks, a tweed sports jacket, a white shirt, and a flame-red tie. He sported a neatly trimmed Van Dyke beard. There was no one else to whom the sports car parked outside could possibly belong.

"Perhaps I can explain what's going on," the man said. His voice was smooth, urbane, sophisticated ... but his words struck like darts.

The muscles along the old man's jaws flexed.

The kid stifled a sigh, a groan of resignation.

The man in the flame-red tie came forward.

The people around him eased away, as though any sort of contact with him might prove fatal.

He said, "The situation is a good deal more complicated than a simple repair job."

"I knew it," the kid said. "Didn't I tell you? It's always a 'good deal more complicated.'"

"Yes, it is," the swami said. "I, too, long for simplicity."

The old man turned to the man in the red tie. "Who are you *this* time?"

The publican said, "He's in charge of code compliance."

"What?!" the old man said, his voice spiking. "I should have known."

"You knew all along," the swami said. "That's why we made the crossing."

"I suppose so," the old man admitted. He turned to the man in the red tie. "Well? Is it true? Are you in charge of code compliance?"

THREE GUYS AND A BAR

"Yes, it's true," the man said. "I'm the building inspector. I'm also responsible for planning and zoning. This building is in violation and must be demolished."

Shouts of outrage stippled the room.

"On what basis?" the kid asked.

"The studs are on twelve-inch centers rather than sixteen. It's the same with the ceiling joists, the floor joists, and the rafters. The foundations are reinforced concrete. Code doesn't allow that." He produced several sheets of paper and handed them to the old man. "As you can see, the list of violations is quite lengthy."

"No doubt," the old man said dryly.

He glanced at the papers and handed them to the kid.

"Not to mention the ravages of time," the inspector said. "Drip, drip, drip. In this climate, time is the great enemy. Rot. Fatigue. It all adds up."

"Time is beside the point," the old man said. "By the way, how did they get tangled up with you in the first place?"

"I offered them my services—building and zoning codes—and they agreed."

"Why would they do such a thing?" the old man asked, no less incredulous than he'd been before. "How'd they ever take it into their heads that they needed building and zoning codes, let alone someone like you to enforce them?"

"You'll have to ask them," the inspector said.

The old man fixed his gaze on the publican. "Well?"

The publican stared at the tabletop. He shrugged, and said, "We were bored. We wanted a bit of a change, a bit of excitement. We had the feeling we were missing out."

The old man returned his attention to the inspector. "I wonder where they got the idea they were missing out?" the old man asked sardonically.

"I am a font of discontent."

"Oh, really? I hadn't noticed," the old man said.

The kid gestured with the sheaf of papers. "This is one heck of a stack," he observed.

"I like to be thorough," the inspector said.

The old man turned back to the publican. "What does 'missing out' have to do with building codes? The instructions we left you don't say anything about building codes."

"Well, we decided we wanted the sign, you know, to dress the place up a little—the sign and a lot of other stuff, actually—and, well, once we started working on it, we got to thinking about what we were doing and about how we couldn't really be sure we were doing the work right—we didn't want to take a chance of ruining the place—and, well, he came along and offered to help."

The building inspector smiled and took a slight bow. "I enjoy lending a hand wherever I'm able."

"And now you people are most assuredly no longer 'missing out,'" the swami said to the publican, to the people in general.

"I'll bet they wish they were," the old man said.

There was an uneasy shuffling of feet, but if anything, the cook's glare grew more intense, more deeply challenging.

"We wish it from the very bottom of our hearts," the publican said.

"It was ever thus," the swami said.

To the publican, the kid said, "You ought to have ignored him."

"Yes," the publican said, "but we didn't."

THREE GUYS AND A BAR

"I told you not to go mountain climbing with him," the kid said.

"Yes," the publican said, "but we did."

"More's the pity," the old man said. "Why'd you do it? Why'd you turn to him for help?"

The people murmured and looked away.

The cook stepped forward. "Because you weren't here," he said. His voice very hard, very loud, and very resentful. "What were we supposed to do?"

"We've been here the whole time," the old man said.

"You could have fooled us," the cook said.

"Well, at least, he is not backing down," the swami observed. "That is something to the good."

The publican said, "What the cook is trying to say is, we never saw you."

"That's because you weren't paying attention," the old man said.

The kid turned back to the top sheet and skimmed forward, slowing to read here and there before hurrying forward again. As he did, his eyes got bigger, then narrowed, and then got bigger again.

"This stuff is a load of crap," the kid said. To the building inspector, he said, "Nothing you've listed here has any effect on the strength and integrity of the building. In fact, this building is stronger than any building that could ever possibly be built to your precious codes."

"Nevertheless," the building inspector said, "it does not comply and must come down."

Renewed gasps and yells of anguish coursed through the room.

THE GREAT MYSTERY OF ETERNITY

The swami smiled reassuringly to the crowd. "Do not be afraid," he said. "All will be well."

"Save your petty reassurances," the inspector said. "This building must come down. They agreed to the codes and to *my* enforcement of them. You have no role here."

"How so?" the old man asked.

"I should think that would be obvious," the inspector said. "They've promised to abide by my rulings."

"Then where are your bulldozers?" the old man asked. "Where are your drop boxes? Where is your crew of wreckers?" Staring hard into the inspectors face, he asked, "Why haven't you already torn it down?"

The inspector stared back into the old man's face. It was as though the inspector were in the grip of some hitherto private triumph, as though he were as yet undecided about allowing anyone else in on the cosmic joke.

"Envy," the swami said, half in speculation and half in declaration. "His motivation has been envy from the start. We built a magnificent building for these people. We did not build it for him—or for his kind—but for *them*. And now his jealousy consumes him."

"Nonsense," the inspector said.

"Yes, it is nonsense," the swami said. "It is utter nonsense, but it is also indisputably true."

The inspector quirked his lip at them. "All right," he said. "It's true." He made a quick gesture that took in the whole room. "Yes, you built it for them, and you turned it over to them, and look at what they've done with it. They've turned its fate over to *me*. Go ahead. Take a good look at what they've done. I want you to see every last bit of it."

THREE GUYS AND A BAR

"I know what they've done," the old man said. "They've made a hideous bargain. With you. But I also know they've used this building as we intended for them to use it. They gather here. They eat, and drink, and talk among themselves. They come here to fall in love, to show off their children, and to mourn their dead."

"Yes, but is that *all* they've done?" the inspector asked. "What about their new sign? What led them to install that abomination ... and to seek my approval for their work?"

"Fear," the swami said.

"Yes! And into what else has their fear led them?"

"No doubt it has led them into all manner of foolishness," the swami said. "We knew it would. We most certainly knew what would transpire even before we moved the first shovelful of dirt. We have always known."

"I'd better have a look," the kid said.

The publican handed him a flashlight. "Don't be surprised at what you find. We've been busy."

"Fear and envy will do that," the kid said.

The inspector handed a booklet to the kid. "Those are the building and zoning codes they've agreed to."

"For this building?" the kid asked.

"Yes, for this building," the inspector said.

The kid pocketed the booklet and left the room.

The sound of the basement door opening and closing filled the room.

Nobody spoke.

The publican sipped his beer. He munched one of his leftover french fries.

When he'd finished, he leaned in close to the old man, and asked, "What *is* he doing here?"

"Don't look at me," the old man said. "You're the ones who invited him in."

"Maybe so, but you three are the ones who've allowed him to run around loose."

"Don't evade. You could have thrown him out whenever you chose to, and you haven't. After all, we entrusted this place to you. It was your responsibility to protect and maintain it."

"Now you're the one who's evading," the publican said. "You've always known how dangerous he is."

"Since when is it my job to do your work for you?"

Interjecting himself into the conversation, the cook said, "More evasion."

The basement door opened and closed, and then the door to the upstairs opened and closed. The kid's footfalls on the stairs thumped through the bar.

"No, it's not really more evasion," the old man said, picking up the thread of the conversation. "These choices are yours to make, not ours." Including both the cook and the publican—and anyone else who cared to join in—the old man asked, "Tell me, what is it you want from us?"

"I, rather, we, all of us, that is, want you to make him go away," the publican said. "We want him to leave us alone."

"What are you willing to trade in exchange?" the old man asked.

"What do you mean?" the cook asked.

"I mean you have to grow up. I mean you have to quit being afraid. You have to make your own decisions, and then live by them."

"You could stop him if you wanted to," the publican said.

"Now you're just being petulant," the old man said. "He

THREE GUYS AND A BAR

makes his own decisions, the same as you."

The door to the upstairs opened and closed, and the kid came back into the room. His face was pale and his jaw muscles had bunched into knots.

He sat down, and the waitress brought him a beer and a bowl of peanuts.

"What did you find?" the old man asked.

"Can't you tell?" the inspector asked.

"I want to hear it from him," the old man said.

The kid sipped his beer. The knotted muscles softened. He munched a handful of peanuts, and the muscles softened further.

"Well," the kid said at last, "I did find several code violations."

The inspector grinned wolfishly.

"However," the kid went on, "none of the violations has weakened the building or creates any sort of danger. Some of their choices wouldn't have been my choices, but they've done nothing inherently wrong, certainly nothing to justify demolition."

Smiles and shouts of assent spread through the room.

"The decision is not yours to make," the inspector said. "The building is in violation; therefore, it must come down."

The publican gave the old man a long, long stare. "It isn't up to *him*, is it? It's up to *us*. We made this contract, and we can break it. We can renounce the whole thing, can't we?"

The old man nodded his head. "Yes, you can."

"No, we must not do that!" a voice from the very back of the room thundered. A man pushed his way forward. His face was the craggy face of a film star, all lines and planes and prominences. He had on hiking clothes, a broad-brimmed hat to ward off the sun, and desert boots.

Addressing the group, the man said, "When these three turned this bar over to us, we promised to take care of it. We gave them our word. But then, we wanted *more*. We lost our confidence in ourselves. We grew afraid that we were 'missing out' on things that we had never wanted before." He pointed at the inspector. "And that's when that *person* offered to step in and solve our problems for us, and that's when we agreed to go back on our word, and that's when we agreed to follow him. We promised to do it, to be loyal to him instead of being loyal to the three."

"What's your point?" the publican demanded.

The man in the hiking clothes drew himself up. "Remember his history." Again, he pointed at the inspector. "At one point, he promised to work for the old man, but then he broke his word and went out and set up his own operation."

"So what?" the publican asked.

"If we go back on our word now, we'll be no better than he is."

"He's right," the cook said. "Another broken promise will only lead to more deceit and more misery."

"Exactly," the hiker said. "If we think we're miserable now, just wait until we've broken our word a second time. There'll be no end to it. The truth will vanish in a paroxysm of expedience. We'll have done exactly what *he* wants us to do."

"But the old man said we could," the publican objected.

"He said we had the ability to do it, not that we ought to do it," the hiker countered.

"Come on," the kid whispered. "You're almost there. Take the next jump. It's been right in front of you the whole time."

"Then what can we do?" the publican asked.

"Nothing," the inspector said. "You can tear down this bar, and if you decide to build another one, you'll have to build it according to *my* building and zoning codes. There's nothing else

THREE GUYS AND A BAR

you can do."

"That's where you're wrong," the hiker said.

"Yes," the kid whispered. "Now the leap."

"Our agreement was for *this* building and *this* building only," the hiker said. He held up a copy of the code booklet.

Here it came.

The hiker opened the booklet and read, "'Therefore, the statutes and regulations set forth herein shall apply to The Earth and to no other structure or structures.' Remember how we included that wording in order to protect our houses and farms." He turned to the inspector. "You agreed to its inclusion because you thought that sooner or later you'd be able to convince us to extend your mandate."

"No doubt that was to have been his price for allowing you to keep The Earth intact," the swami said. "He knows how important this place is to you. He is fully aware that you would do anything to hold on to it. He knew that all he had to do was stampede you into granting him his fondest desire: complete and irrevocable control."

The look on the inspector's face betrayed that the swami had hit the mark. In turn, that mark explained why the inspector had not unleashed his demolition team.

The hiker said to the building inspector, "We gave you power over *this* building. You'll have no power whatsoever over any subsequent building we may or may not choose to build."

"Good for you," the kid whispered. "You've made the jump."

"Indeed," the swami said, "and with no more from us than a little judicious prodding."

The old man shrugged. "Well, we did have to make the crossing. And in that miserable fog, too."

THE GREAT MYSTERY OF ETERNITY

"Oh, yes," the swami said, "I'd forgotten about the fog."

To the people in general, the publican said, "It's time for us to grow up and get to work."

~~*

Over the next several days, the fog gradually lifted.

The hiker and the publican lead the people in the dismantling of The Earth. They brought in backhoes, scoop loaders, and dump trucks. They hauled away everything, right down to the concrete and rebar used in the foundation.

The people had expected the building inspector to leave, but he hung on, watching the work. He even took a hand from time to time, pulling this down, helping to load that for its trip to the landfill.

Some said it showed that he wasn't such a bad fellow, after all, and that maybe he'd changed; but others said that it only showed he wasn't the sort to take no for an answer, that if bullying hadn't worked—which it nearly had—then perhaps soft-soap would.

Once the site was clear, the kid helped them draw up the plans for a new bar. The people called it The New Earth.

Then they excavated for the new foundation, right down to the bedrock. With that job out of the way, they built the forms, set the rebar in place, and poured the concrete.

~~*

One morning, the sun burned off the very last of the fog.

The three guys announced it was time for them to set sail.

THREE GUYS AND A BAR

They said good-bye up at the site of the new bar, sharing in the excitement as the forms were knocked away from the new foundation.

Then, alone, they went down to their ketch.

The building inspector was waiting for them on the dock. He was wearing his signature white shirt and flame-red tie.

"I came to wish you a pleasant journey," the inspector said. "I hope you don't mind."

"Why should we?" the old man asked.

"I nearly scored this time," the inspector said.

"We don't bear grudges," the old man said.

"Still ...."

"Say what you have to say," the old man said.

"It was a near-run thing. Well played. You have my congratulations."

"It was no game," the kid said. "Besides, you ought to congratulate *them*." He nodded up towards the construction site. "They're the ones who routed you."

The inspector smiled most benignly. "Have they?"

"They have," the old man said.

The swami added, "Most assuredly."

The inspector shrugged, as though admitting the point. For now. "As you say."

"We do say," the kid said.

The old man went aboard, unlocked the cabin, and started the engine. Meanwhile, the kid and the swami took in the spring lines and singled up the bow and stern lines.

"See you again soon," the inspector said, and gave them a little wave.

"I look forward to it," the old man said, his voice pitched to carry above the rumble of the boat's diesel.

The old man gave the order, and the kid and swami took in the bow and stern lines.

The old man dropped the transmission into reverse and slowly backed the boat away from the dock.

The inspector watched them pull away, watched the kid and the swami take in the fenders, watched the old man swing the boat around and head out into the bay, a bay that might have been just about anywhere along the Sunshine Coast of British Columbia.

The kid looked back, back at the inspector. He was watching them.

"He isn't leaving," the kid said.

"He will once he gets tired of watching us," the old man said.

"That's not what I meant," the kid said.

"I know it isn't," the old man said. "He'll never leave them alone."

"Envy will do that," the kid said.

The old man edged the throttle forward a trifle.

The engine's note changed and the boat's speed increased. She picked up the first real swells, the first lazy swells, coming in from the outside.

Overhead the sun shone in a blue sky, and they had the promise of a good breeze. It was perfect sailing weather.

"One of us ought to stay behind," the kid said.

The three of them fell silent for a time.

Finally, the swami said, "I'll do it. Either of you would only intimidate them, whereas I can move about among them unnoticed and unremarked, helping here, encouraging there, rescuing from time to time. Agreed?"

THREE GUYS AND A BAR

"It's your call," the old man said.

"Fine by me, if that's how you want it," the kid said.

The swami closed his eyes, and an expression of intense concentration settled onto his face.

After an extended moment, the expression cleared, and the swami opened his eyes. "Done," he said. "I will now be present there without interruption—there and wherever else I choose to be."

The kid shook his head. "How do you do that?" he asked.

"As I have tried so very many times to explain—"

"All right, knock it off, you two," the old man said. "It's about time we turned this floating lovely into a sailboat."

The kid and the swami stowed the fenders and the docking lines. They took in the sail covers and made sure the halyards and sheets were free to run properly.

Meanwhile, the boat crossed out of the bay and into the water outside, out onto a wide, windswept expanse.

The kid looked back at the entrance. There, perched on the rocks on each side, dozens of cormorants held out their wings, drying them.

"We'll have to go back there," he said. "We'll have to do it all over again, or something very like it."

"You saved the waypoints, did you not?" the swami asked the old man.

In reply, the old man pointed at the side of his head. "Thoroughly memorized."

He looked at the bright blue sky, the set of the swells, their tops just beginning to shatter into whitecaps, and listened to the song of the wind in the rigging.

"Come on, lads," the old man said. "Jump to it. There's sailing to be done!"

THE SECOND MATE'S CUP OF TEA

It's Queen Victoria's seventy-first birthday, and a proper Englishman find himself far from home and homesick. All he wants is a cup of English tea. Served properly. On clean china. On clean table linen. In a clean dining room. However, in the small lumber port of Garibaldi, Oregon, such amenities can be hard to find. And thereby hangs a tale.

THE HONOURABLE ALBERT WILLIAM GEORGE FREDERICK RATHBONE, an Englishman and second mate of the *Santianna*, a Pacific Coast lumber schooner, sat alone at a small, square table. The table sported a dirty white cloth and occupied a dark corner in the dining room of the Grand Mariner Hotel in Garibaldi, Oregon.

Garibaldi held pride of place as one of the smaller lumber-and-fishing ports on the Oregon coast. In point of dismal fact, if the entrance to Tillamook Bay, and thus to Garibaldi, had been any worse, there wouldn't have been any grand mariners to patronize the hotel named in their honor, not sane ones, anyway.

Sane.

Rathbone turned the word over in his mind. When it came right down to it, would any sane man go to work in the lumber fleet in the first place, especially if he were qualified for grander things? A steamer, say?

Possibly.

More often than not, lumber schooners worked coastwise. This meant that their crews could enjoy reasonable home lives.

Moreover, the ships tended to embrace informal ways of getting the job done, and their crews touted them as great *feeders*. Unless bound for a long voyage—out into the Pacific, say—they had no reason to shanghai anyone and almost never did.

Nevertheless, despite their charms, it remained unlikely that anyone with the qualifications for grander employment wouldn't leave the doughty lumber haulers and their weather-bound coasts behind.

Without a doubt, Rathbone was qualified for better things, more lucrative things, more noteworthy things, both by training and by influence, but here he was, working in the West Coast's lumber fleet, the so-called Scandinavian Navy due to the disproportionate numbers of Norwegians and Swedes in the fleet. And why was Rathbone so serving? For his sins, naturally. Old sins, forgotten sins, but so far they had remained resolutely indelible.

Admittedly, as noted, the work did have its attractions; however, Rathbone could not say that the Grand Mariner Hotel was to be found among them.

From the outside, the establishment looked as though someone had piled up a half dozen millworker's cottages in a pile two deep and three high, and had then tied them all together with a false front and a single coat of yellow paint. The trim was green.

From the inside, the hotel appeared to be pretentious and unkempt, as though the cottages were about to disassociate themselves from one another and go their separate ways. Or perhaps it was more as if brooms, dustpans, and paintbrushes were in short supply.

The dining room offered its own unique charm. All around Rathbone swirled the offensive odors of greasy American food, the stench of poorly trimmed kerosene lamps, and the clank and clink of abused cutlery and china. The nasal braying, shouts, and guffaws that passed for conversation pulsed in the fetid air. At times the reports actually echoed from the walls and windows.

The date was May 24, 1890, the Queen's seventy-first birthday, and at the moment, Rathbone, an English aristocrat through and through, felt very far away from the civilities of hearth and home, his *English* hearth and home.

The truth be told, he felt acutely distant from a decent, respectable cup of tea.

Ten minutes ago, the waitress, a razor-thin girl with oily, brown hair and dull-brown eyes, had crowded a teapot and the other tea things onto his table. She had then stared at him as though he were a madman, as though she expected him to foam at the mouth and rave at the top of his lungs.

She was wearing a white shirtwaist and a gray skirt. The shirtwaist had egg and gravy stains on it, while the skirt had a wilted, unpressed look.

Not only her clothes, but her fingernails were grimy, too. Could it be that her father was a locomotive mechanic and that she helped him work on the engines when she wasn't waiting on tables?

He asked, "Is that really tea in the pot? Not watered-down coffee, but actual tea?"

One of the restaurants he'd ventured into up in Hoquiam had attempted to make tea by steeping coffee beans in hot water. The result wasn't undrinkable, but it was also neither tea nor coffee.

"Yes, sir, it's tea," the waitress said. Her dull-brown eyes narrowed. "I know the difference."

"Do you? How commendable."

She glared at him, and said, "Thank you, sir. I hope you enjoy your *tea*, sir."

He had then thanked her for the *tea*, and she had begrudgingly taken the rest of his order. She'd scribbled furiously on her pad with the stub of a yellow pencil. That done, she'd hurried off toward the kitchen.

Tea.

Yes, well .... Rathbone could tell from the odor rising from the pot that the beverage she'd served him was nothing of the sort.

It never was, especially in these small, coastal towns. Most of them were no better than sawmills with a few houses, a few brothels, a few saloons, and a dock attached. In the genuine doghole ports down in Northern California, down along the Redwood Coast, there weren't even docks.

There were always saloons, brothels, and opium dens—business is business—but never any genuine tea.

Unlike tea, opium and prostitutes held no allure for Rathbone. His father, the 15th baron of Hornsea, had died of syphilis, and his younger brother was a dissipated opium eater. His older brother, the heir, was fond of cocaine, which he injected to no good effect.

So much for prostitutes and drugs.

As for saloons, Rathbone found them to be, well, not worth the bother. On those rare occasions when he wanted to drink himself into a fit of vomiting and unconsciousness, he much preferred to buy a bottle of Scotch and take it back to the ship. If he were going to pass out somewhere, he'd choose a scupper over a gutter any old day.

All of which led to his unending quest for a drinkable cup of tea. Call him an eccentric, call him a loon, but while most men went ashore looking for easy women and cheap booze, he went

THE SECOND MATE'S CUP OF TEA

ashore looking for English tea and English scones.

Seattle came close to making authentic tea; San Francisco closer still. But even they fell short of the mark. Portland's notion of tea was primitive at best. They made tea as though they'd read the instructions in a New York Times' article and had believed every word.

Rathbone allowed that group of ideas, that collection of disgruntled musings, to settle, rather as one might allow tea leaves to settle to the bottom of a pot, or allow a bottle of wine to breathe.

After all these years, why did Rathbone still make the attempt? Why did he insist, no matter where the ship was either taking on or discharging cargo, on searching out the town's best restaurant and ordering tea?

The answers swirled up around him like waterspouts.

Hope. Stubbornness. An unwillingness to accept that he was out of place in the place he had chosen to be.

And so it was that at this very moment Bertie Rathbone found himself with nothing better to do than drink his tea and wait for his supper to arrive. And to contemplate the vagaries of a country that did not take tea at four o'clock in the afternoon and that ate supper (or dinner, according to some) as close to six o'clock in the afternoon as possible.

Scones, or something like scones, were called biscuits, biscuits were called cookies, and the ground floor was called the first floor. Public schools were schools that were run by the government rather than schools that were merely open to the public. And a universal effort was apparently underway to drop the letter *u* from as many words as possible, resulting in such spellings as *color* rather than *colour* and *labor* rather than *labour* and *harbor* rather than *harbour*. The list of these American cultural temper tantrums was as good as endless.

It had to be the fault of the coffee: coffee with breakfast, coffee at midmorning, coffee with dinner (or lunch, depending), coffee in the middle of the afternoon, coffee with or after supper (or dinner, depending), and even coffee before bed.

Rathbone was certain his list was missing any number of other times at which the vile, caustic brew was consumed.

On the other hand, given the quality of the tea in America, it was understandable that coffee would be the beverage of choice.

Aboard ship they drank coffee, of course, especially when they could afford to lay in a supply from a shop called Arabian Coffee and Spice Mills in San Francisco. When they couldn't, they had to settle for whatever the thieving chandlers sent them, or whatever they could find in whichever port they were in when they ran out, or whatever they could buy or beg from other ships.

Be that as it may, no matter what they were drinking aboard ship, they went through gallons of it. Cookie's brew was "strong enough to float an egg", although, as far as Rathbone knew, no one had ever tried to float an egg in it. No doubt the egg would dissolve long before it ever had a chance to sink.

But coffee aboard ship was supposed to be different. It was a stimulant, not a beverage. Aboard ship, coffee was an essential part of getting the job done. It was not one of the vanishing social graces, not an island of sanity in an insane world, not an anchor connecting him to a life he would never see again, one he regretted not living.

And so here he was, looking for an honest pot of tea, and perfectly willing to find it, but without any real hope of doing so ... despite the hotel's local reputation.

THE SECOND MATE'S CUP OF TEA

The Grand Mariner Hotel and its dining room were said to be the best Garibaldi had to offer. The only other town within reach was Tillamook, but that was too far to go.

It was absolutely no use complaining. Acceptance was Rathbone's only alternative.

There had to be a Latin or Greek saying that covered the situation, a saying that his classics teachers had drilled into him, but try as he might, he couldn't bring it to mind.

No, until they'd finished loading—a deck cargo of pilings for San Francisco—he was stuck right where he was. He could either eat aboard the good ship *Santianna* or he could eat at the Grand Mariner.

He was sick of the food aboard, but even before he'd tasted any of it, Rathbone was sick of the food at the Grand Mariner.

Fried grease and dirty fingernails. For those, he may as well have turned his palate over to Cookie.

Rathbone stared morosely into his empty cup. The waitress hadn't filled it and neither had he.

He didn't want to fill it, but he knew damn good and well that he would.

What he wanted to do was to quit hiding and go home, home to order, civility, and *English* tea. Home to being the second son of a baron instead of the second mate of a three-masted lumber schooner.

The teapot was close at hand, but he did not reach for it. So, too, was the milk pitcher. The sugar bowl. The cup. The saucer. Everything was there, except for a cozy. Evidently, the Grand Mariner's sense of unrivaled elegance didn't reach as far as tea cozies.

He looked at the tea things, took them in as a whole, and

felt even farther away from England than he had just moments before.

The problem was that none of the tea things matched. The cup was white, while its saucer was pale yellow and didn't fit the cup. The teapot was pattered in blue on white (a fox-hunting scene), the milk pitcher in red on white (a view of London's Tower Bridge), and the sugar bowl had a purple-and-green floral pattern. The pieces were obviously not part of a set, but had been brought together to fulfill a purpose, each snatched in haste from a catchall cupboard.

They were, Rathbone decided, tokens of the wages of sin: not death, but an existence in the wilderness.

In all honesty, however, the cream pitcher and the cup might have once been quite lovely. Now they were chipped, cracked, and discolored. Now they were odds and ends. Now they were too useful to throw away, but not good enough to treat with care.

Like the *Santianna*, like her crew, like Rathbone himself: they were aging, nearly used up.

Aging?

Rathbone was only thirty-six. He was far from aging, and he was farther still from used up.

Still, thirty-six was rather old for a second mate. And he was English, an Englishman employed in an American trade dominated by Scandinavians. Squareheads, as they were ubiquitously called.

There were days when Rathbone felt as though he were the object of a vast xenophobic malevolence, as though the American Revolution and the War of 1812 had happened only yesterday.

Well, all he could say on that score was, Thank God for the Empire in general and Canada in particular!

THE SECOND MATE'S CUP OF TEA

Rathbone seized the teapot and filled his cup.

The liquid was brown. It looked like tea, but it smelt like boiled weeds, like tannin-rich runoff that had been allowed to age to perfection and then strained and heated over a kerosene stove.

The milk itself looked and smelt as though it might have come from a cow sometime within the last month. It was not spoiled. It poured readily. It did not curdle when it mixed with the tea. He took these for three good signs.

The sugar, however, looked and smelt as though it had begun life as something else. Just what that might have been, Rathbone found it hard to imagine.

Whatever the case, the sugar could not be spooned from the bowl. He had to break it loose with a table knife and dump the resulting lumps into the cup.

Rathbone lifted the cup to his lips.

God only knew how his food would turn out. The very air had a slick, unwashed feel to it. Thick. Oily. Unwholesome. Confined.

He wanted desperately to be at sea again.

He sipped the tea.

His lips snapped back from the cup as though a wasp had stung them. They carried the rest of his face in their wake.

"Bloody hell!"

Heads turned in his direction.

He felt himself blush. He grinned in embarrassment and stared down at his cup.

He wasn't quite sure what he'd expected, but it hadn't been a brew that tasted as though it had been made by steeping a mixture of rose-bush clippings and dandelion leaves in hot water.

THE GREAT MYSTERY OF ETERNITY

No doubt it was one of the local favorites: an herbal concoction served by the local Grange ladies. The Grange? That *was* the name of the organization, wasn't it? Yes, that was it: the Grange.

What sort of group was it, again?

He'd been told, but he couldn't quite remember. Farming, wasn't it? Hated the railroads and the banks, didn't they? It only made sense that they would. Farmers always hated the railroads and the banks. The railroads routinely gouged, and the banks acted as though they owned everything in sight, including their customers. It was positively feudal. A subject about which Rathbone, being the second son of a baron, knew a thing or three.

The tea was execrable, but he would, alas, have to make do.

The waitress reappeared at his table. Her hair was coming loose from its pins in a couple of places. No doubt she combed it with kipper backbones.

"Is everything all right?" she asked.

"Why wouldn't it be?" Rathbone asked.

"You caused a disturbance."

"Oh, that. I was surprised. I cried out without thinking. Been at sea too long. Won't happen again."

"I hope not," she said. "How'd the tea turn out?"

"The tea? It's adequate."

The girl's eyes went large, and she hurried away. To Rathbone, it looked as though she'd *run* out to the kitchen. That, however, would have been impossible. No establishment as pretentious as the Grand Mariner would so much as *think* of allowing one of its employees to run under any circumstances.

Rathbone sipped his tea.

More than once in his life, he had at first despised something only to find out later that he rather liked it. He couldn't remember an instance offhand, but he was sure there had to have been one. His school? His college? The new cook—the redoubtable Mrs. Fitzgerald, the year he'd turned twelve. No, he'd hated the lot of them from start to finish, and the Grand Mariner's tea was proving to be no exception.

A man with a decidedly middle-class managerial bearing—part arrogance and part subservience—approached his table. The man was tall and wide through the shoulders and hips. He was tending to fat. Yes, he had a lot of weight, but he also had very little effective muscle. He was dressed in an ill-cut suit, and held his lips slightly pursed, as though he'd just discovered a chamber pot that hadn't been emptied in several days.

Rathbone knew the type—pompous, self-important, overbearing, pretentious, and stubborn; and of all the types on offer he despised it the most.

For one thing, it reminded him too much of many of the members of his family, not that his family worked in restaurants. Far from it. No, they were high enough on the social ladder to imagine that with a bit of luck and the right social coup they might be called upon to serve as ladies in waiting, or as private secretaries in the royal household, or as what amounted to the managers of one or another of the lesser royal estates.

However, they were decidedly *not* high enough on the social ladder for any of it to ever in fact happen. Oh, well, there was always next year, the next decade, the next generation. What the family needed was a couple of generals or admirals to set them right. To recapture their once proud position. I say, Charlie, you like to sail. Why don't you give it a go, what?

"Good afternoon," the fat man in the ill-fitting suit said. His voice was as oily as the girl's hair.

THE GREAT MYSTERY OF ETERNITY

The dining-room manager. Like as not, he called himself the *maître d'*. Like as not, he forced everyone else to refer to him as the *maître d'*. He'd probably come down from Portland hoping to make it big in the boom-and-bust resort business. The Oregon Coast was littered with planned resorts, resorts under construction, new resorts, failing resorts, and failed resorts. The hint of a rail connection was enough to send land prices skyrocketing, fueled by the illusion of those teeming tens of thousands from Portland, Salem, Corvallis, and Eugene who wanted nothing quite so much as to hike on the sand, collect agates, and devour baked clams—in the cold and the year-round rain.

"Good afternoon," Rathbone said.

The man raised his eyebrows expectantly. "Is something wrong? I understand you've been boisterous and rude to the waitress."

Rude? Rathbone was willing to admit to sarcastic, but not to rude. These people hadn't seen rude. The second son of a baron could attain heights of rudeness these yokels couldn't envisage, no matter how filthy or drunk they happened to be.

"I don't understand," Rathbone said as pleasantly as he good. "Is the tea not to your liking?"

The *tea*? Rathbone wished to Heaven they'd served him tea.

"What tea would that be?" Rathbone asked.

A managerial eyebrow shot up. "The tea Amanda served you."

"Ah, that remarkable beverage in the pot," Rathbone said. "So that's what you call it: *tea*. How unspeakably quaint."

Rathbone stood. He was acting on impulse now, behaving against his better judgment, against his training, against his upbringing. On the other hand, what did they bloody well expect?

THE SECOND MATE'S CUP OF TEA

To be able to serve him any old swill and have him smile sweetly and guzzle it down and pay for it without so much as a mild protest? How much of their sneering incompetence was he supposed to put up with? No, he'd had enough, and the last thing he was about to tolerate was a tongue lashing from a jumped-up toad.

Rathbone snatched an empty water glass from the neighboring table and poured the remaining contents of his tea cup into it.

"Say, what are you doing?" the manager asked.

"Patience, my good man. Patience. All is soon to be revealed."

Rathbone filled the newly emptied cup from the pot on his table. He set it in a saucer and handed them to the manager.

"What am I supposed to do with this?" the man asked.

"You're supposed to taste it and then tell me whether or not it *is* tea. You see, your question—'Is the tea not to your liking?'—presupposes that what Amanda served me is truly a pot of tea. I maintain that it is not. I told her it was 'adequate' out of politeness. You are another case altogether."

"Say, what are you trying to pull?"

"Pull? Me? Nothing. I was not served tea. I was served a pot of hot water into which had been infused a mixture of black tea, assorted garden clippings, various herbs, dandelion leaves, rose hips, and, if I'm not mistaken, ground opium seed pods."

The manager grew red in the face. "Opium—"

Rathbone raised a silencing hand. "No doubt this concoction is all the local rage; nevertheless, it is not *tea*."

"You were rude to Amanda!"

Rathbone had kept his voice down. He could have rattled the windows if he had chosen to do so, but after his initial outburst, he'd decided to leave his reefed-topsails bellow aboard ship.

The manager had not.

The dining room fell silent.

"I was not rude. I was not so much as unpleasant. Amanda is an unwashed nincompoop, and your establishment is a fraud. Shall I continue? I'm perfectly capable."

"You son of a bitch!" the manager said, and with that, he took a swing at Rathbone's jaw.

Unfortunately for the manager, Rathbone had attended one of the more rough-and-tumble public schools. With the ease of one swatting away a fruit fly, Rathbone blocked the punch, moved in, and landed a solid blow on the man's nose.

The manager staggered back. Blood flowed down over his mouth.

Having no desire to continue the fight, Rathbone did not press his advantage. Rather, he stood calmly where he was, but with his fits raised, waiting to meet out whatever was called for. The message ought to have been clear enough to even the most provincial of opportunists.

But it wasn't.

The manager balled his hands into fists and ran at Rathbone. *Ran*!

Rathbone pivoted out of the way, rather like a matador, he thought, and landed a blow on the back of the manager's neck.

The man staggered, but did not go down.

Rathbone, ever the gentleman, held his position. Back at school, he would have thrown himself onto the fellow, driving him down in a hail of blows and kicks. Those more civilized days were over, except on those rare occasions when a member of the crew got his hands on a particularly nasty batch of liquor and went temporarily chemically insane.

THE SECOND MATE'S CUP OF TEA

The manager bellowed a few incomprehensible curses, and charged.

Where had the man learned to fight?

Wherever it had been, he ought to return and demand a refund of his tuition.

This time, Rathbone planted his feet and addressed himself to the inept attack.

The manager closed, but just as Rathbone was about to land a serious blow to the man's jaw, a hand clamped down on Rathbone's shoulder and pulled him away. Simultaneously, the newcomer came around from behind and used his other hand to push the manager off to one side.

The manager flailed to a stop and stared at the newcomer. "What'd you do that for, Frank?"

Amanda stood behind the newcomer, Frank. Her eyes were wide with fright, which, paradoxically, made them look even beadier than they had before.

Frank was tall, taller than Rathbone, and he was wide through the shoulders, narrow through the hips. No paunch. He had on a dark suit and a derby hat. A policeman's shield was pinned to his jacket, and a policeman's glower was pinned to his face.

Apparently, Amanda had run out for help.

"I'll take it from here, Augie," Frank said.

"I was doing just fine," Augie said.

"You were *doing just fine* at getting your ass whupped."

Augie glared at the cop, but he didn't say anything.

"I'll do what's needful," Frank said.

Augie looked down at the deck.

It was clear as could be who ran the town, and it wasn't Augie. Frank turned to Rathbone. "Garibaldi don't hold with your sort causin' trouble in respectable establishments. You wanna get out of line, you'll have to go on down to The Happy Mermaid."

Rathbone rolled his eyes. The Happy Mermaid. That name *had* to be the product of yet another Portland refugee seeking his fortune among the crab pots and clam shovels.

"My *sort*? And what *sort* would my sort be?"

"The sort that likes to cause trouble."

"I beg to differ. My sort is the sort who would like to just once order a cup of tea in this benighted country and to be served a cup of honest-to-goodness tea and not the lukewarm runoff from the nearest cow pasture."

"You don't think much of us hicks, do you?"

"No, now you mention it, I can't say I do."

"Well, now, just about makes us even. I can't say I think much of your kind, either."

He pronounced the word *ee-thur*. It was another Americanism, sort of. Prince Albert, being German, had pronounced the word *eye-thur*, and because he had, England had taken to pronouncing it that way, too. America, naturally, had stuck with *ee-thur*—the adolescent twits.

Frank leaned in close, eyes narrowed, jaw set.

Rathbone had knocked too many policemen's helmets off too many policemen's heads to be intimidated.

He did not shrink back. Instead, he leaned in toward Frank.

The man smelled of cigars, sausage, and damp wool.

Frank said, "Maybe your majesty will think more highly of our hick jail."

"Do you intend to arrest me?"

"Ain't no *intend* about it. I just did," Frank said, his voice pitched low, no better than a primal growl.

THE SECOND MATE'S CUP OF TEA

"On what charge?" Rathbone demanded.

Again, Frank closed his hand on Rathbone's shoulder. "Disturbing the peace. Vagrancy. Assault. Impersonating Little Lord Fauntleroy." Frank tightened his grip.

"Remove you hand from my shoulder."

Frank pushed down and tightened his grip another notch. "That does it," Frank said. "Maybe a night in jail'll straighten you out."

Rathbone couldn't go to jail, not for the night, not for a couple of hours. *Santianna* was loading and he was needed to do his share overseeing the work ... and doing a good share of it himself too. The ship was two hands short and it was also up to him to find replacements. That meant countless hours scrounging through saloons, flophouses, and, maybe, just maybe, hanging around the sawmills looking for people willing to give up the smell of sawdust for the allure of saltwater.

No, it was all very well and good for locals to stick together and make life difficult for John Bull, but right now, John Bull simply couldn't afford to indulge them.

Nor was he in any mood to be manhandled.

Luckily, Rathbone had been to public school and university. He had served in the Royal Navy. He was currently employed in the merchant service, specifically in the hard-drinking, hard-fighting Scandinavian Navy.

He dropped the shoulder with Frank's hand welded to it, turned, drove his free shoulder into his opponent's chest, and simultaneously buried his elbow in his stomach.

It was a fine start.

And it *ought* to have worked.

THE GREAT MYSTERY OF ETERNITY

~~*

Frank locked Rathbone in one of the two cells in the Garibaldi police station.

Looking out through the bars, Rathbone asked, "Where'd you learn to throw a punch like that?"

"Logging camps mostly."

That explained a lot.

"What happens now?"

"When's your ship leaving?"

"The minute we're loaded," Rathbone said.

Frank nodded.

Rathbone could almost see the wheels turning in the space behind the policeman's eyes. If the ship's second mate were behind bars, the work would take just that much longer to finish.

Frank said, "I'll let you out in the morning."

"Fair enough."

Frank opened the office door. "I'll send Ellen over with some supper."

~~*

A few minutes later, the door swung open and a woman breezed in.

"You must be fairly parched, sir," she said. "I'm Ellen, by the way. Frank's wife."

"Bertie Rathbone, second mate of the *Santianna*."

"Pleased to meet you, sir."

Ellen was Frank's age or a little younger. She had the solid, ruddy look of a woman who's worked hard all her life. Farming,

THE SECOND MATE'S CUP OF TEA

flunkying in logging camps, clerking, cooking, keeping house, chasing after kids—the possibilities cascaded down through Rathbone's mind.

What transfixed him, however, was the tray she carried.

It was silver and on it sat a tea service. The teapot, creamer, sugar bowl, cup, and saucer matched. They were in an ornate flowed pattern, one that was without a doubt English in origin. There was a plate of triangular sandwiches with the crusts cut off and a second plate of biscuits. Cookies, rather. And there was even a silver tea strainer!

The heady aroma of black Chinese tea filled the room.

Ellen was all smiles.

"Frank told me about the trouble you had over at the Grand Mariner."

She had a thoroughly American accent, but there was a lilt to it, a hint in the way she'd said *about*, in the way the pitch rose and fell through *Grand Mariner*.

She set the tray on the desk and opened the cell door. "You can have your tea at Frank's desk. Don't tell Frank. He'd skin me alive if he knew I'd let you out."

"My lips are sealed," Rathbone said, and sat down.

"I don't mean to gossip, but just between us, you didn't give Augie a tenth of what he deserves. The way he puts on airs, and in a town like this; he's asking for a bloody nose. Well, go on, sir, try it. I'm dying to find out what you think of it."

Rathbone felt his stomach sink, but he smiled as appreciatively as he could. The sandwiches and cookies at least looked delicious.

He poured a little cream into the cup, which was spotlessly clean, positioned the strainer, and poured the tea in on top of the cream. Then he added a level spoonful of sugar and stirred it in.

The aroma was heavenly and reminded him of lazy afternoons at Bridgeport Abbey. The abbey, which at one time had been a genuine abbey, was the family's manor house, if it could be called that, on what passed for the family's country estate, which in turn, was nothing but a glorified farm. And not a very lucrative one, at that. It was no wonder the future baron injected himself with cocaine. No wonder their father was in his middle fifties and didn't look a day over seventy-five.

An expression of nervous expectation lit Ellen's face.

Rathbone decided that no matter how ghastly the tea turned out to be, which it surely would, he would praise it to the high heavens.

"It's been several years, sir, since ...," Ellen said, allowing her voice to trail off.

Rathbone lifted the cup. "Here goes," he said.

He sipped.

The tea exploded through his mouth, his brain, his very being.

Any need for pretense instantly evaporated.

The tea was an island of warmth on cold winter evenings.

It was breakfast with his mother and father and brothers.

It was better than that first cup of coffee on dark, cold, wet mornings at sea, before the sun was up.

It was afternoons in London with his girlfriends.

It was a good book by a comfortable fire late at night, with the house quiet and the only sounds the rustling crackle of the flames and the chiming of the grandfather clock out in the hallway.

He was smiling so broadly the muscles in his face ached.

"Where did you learn to make *tea*?" he asked.

"Sir?" she asked, suddenly worried.

THE SECOND MATE'S CUP OF TEA

"No, no, don't misunderstand. It's absolutely wonderful. I haven't had tea this excellent since I left England. Where on earth did you learn how to do it?"

Her smile was as sunny as a clear day in August.

"Why, sir, I was in service up in Victoria, British Columbia for going on ten years." She bobbed a mock curtsey. "That's where I learned how."

Which explained the tea *and* her delightful trace of an accent. He drank off another long sip. He hadn't imagined any of it. The tea was just as excellent as it had been at first.

"When was that? When were you in service?"

"Before I met Frank. He was logging up near Port Alberni, and ... Well, the rest, sir, as they say is history."

"Well, Canada's loss is Oregon's gain," Rathbone said.

She blushed.

"You're welcome, sir." She added, "I'd best leave you to it. I'll be back in a while with your supper."

And then she was gone.

Bertie Rathbone refilled his cup and looked out the police station's front window.

The night was closing in, darkest toward the hills to the east, brighter out over the bay. He could see the tops of *Santianna*'s masts. The sun shone on them, the end of the ship's own special rainbow.

He leaned back in Frank's office chair, drank more of Ellen's tea, *English* tea that she had learned to brew in Canada, and for the first time in years, for the first time since he'd left the Royal Navy and England—in utter disgrace—the Honourable Albert William George Frederick Rathbone felt perfectly and blissfully at home.

MARINA DOGFISH CHOW

Living on a boat in a cozy marina has its rewards. Often the neighbor's dog is not one of them. In the marina featured in this short thriller, B Row is the sort of place that liveaboards can call home and that their dogs would be wise to treat with the utmost respect. Why? Because B Row is the sort place where the unexpected is commonplace.

RICHARD PHILBRICK lived on a 41' cutter three slips farther along B Row from me. His cutter wasn't much of a boat, being one of the Taiwan specials that had definitely not come from one of the better yards. Puget Sound is littered with them, and the yards make a fortune keeping them in repair for "one more season."

Then again, our marina wasn't much of a marina, being south of the Tacoma Narrows; B Row wasn't much of a row, being populated mostly by semi-impoverished liveaboards, and Dick wasn't much of a guy, being possessed of a caustic streak.

In other words, Dick lived up to his nickname—not always but often enough to make life miserable and interesting at the same time.

He was imaginative, though.

The summer that year was hot, by Puget Sound standards, and that evening three of us liveaboards had circled our deckchairs on the headwalk.

The headwalk formed the spine from which finger walks projected at right angles, forming our slips, those chunks of water that each of us called home. Two boats shared a single finger walk, which meant that the spaces *between* the fingers was occupied by two boats, in our marina, anyway. Yes, this will turn out to be important later on.

The three of us were drinking beer and bitching about the local boatyard, about how miserably hot the weather was, about how since Alice's had closed there wasn't a decent restaurant within walking distance, and about how we all were about ready for rain. Sunshine was okay, but even the concrete was looking parched.

Back in the day, docks were made out of logs and planks. These days they are made out of concrete floats.

But I digress.

Needless to say, a good rain would have gone a long way toward cleaning up the ground-in, dried-on seagull, heron, and dog shit.

And speaking of dogs, the dogs were miserable, too. They were bored, irritable, and lethargic. You could tell they were all of those things by the way they gravitated toward their water bowls and by the way they didn't bother pissing on the gate at the top of the ramp. They still tagged the deck boxes and the power stanchions, which were provided for each mooring space, and the fresh-water hose bibs, which were also provided for each space.

In the whole panoply of doggy-pissing targets the hose bibs were the only ones from which we filled our fresh-water tanks, from which, that is, we drew our potable water.

I often daydreamed about hooking up a spark coil to my hose bib, but I invariably talked myself out of it.

Looking back on what happened I wish I hadn't.

It would have been kinder.

MARINA DOGFISH CHOW

Anyway, Dick Philbrick, Ralph Slocum, and I were the three, and Dick and Ralph had their dogs with them, Haimish and Cosmo, respectively.

Ralph lived on a fly-bridge Matthews, a real classic: forty feet of wood and glass, almost none of which was original, including the fastenings. Ralph was a former community-college teacher who'd taken early retirement. I can't recall what he'd taught, but he'd put in his time and boogied.

Dick, by the way, wasn't retired. He owned his own business. He looked after motel-and-hotel Wi-Fi networks, and he did the same for what used to be called internet cafes. It was a decent-enough gig, and he made good money, but he had no real schedule. He worked when they called him, or when he could scare up work to do, day or night. Mostly nights, come to think of it.

Me? I'm a failed wannabe electrical engineer turned trust-fund brat. The trust fund isn't lavish, but I'm not a big spender. I can't afford to be.

Dick and Ralph always had their dogs with them.

They were small dogs and hardly any trouble, apart from the yapping and pissing. Ralph's dog looked like a miniature mutt of the border-collie/miniature Chow variety of bred-small dogs, while Dick's dog might have been a miniature Scotty, if such a breed exists. I suppose it does, because there was the dog and it looked like a Scotty and it was smaller than most of the Scotties I'd seen.

Pissing.

Haimish tagged the deck boxes and power stanchions, but Cosmo delighted in marking the deck boxes, the power stanchions, *and* any hose bib that happened to be in the wrong place at the wrong time.

THE GREAT MYSTERY OF ETERNITY

An instinctive competition exists between dogs to mark territory, and, the truth be told, Cosmo, who was Ralph's dog, and Hamish, who was Dick's dog, were *not* the only two liveaboard dogs on the row, and they certainly weren't the only two dogs who saved up to tag things.

I was one of the scant few on the row who didn't have a dog.

The hose-bib tagging was bad enough in the winter time, but toward the end of summer, if I didn't scrub away the dog piss my section of the headwalk stank.

Some airhead once pointed out to Dick that "it" was "organic."

Dick pointed out to the airhead that cobra venom, syphilis, and cholera were also organic.

That earned Dick an outraged glare, the sort reserved for the hopelessly unenlightened, for those who had not had their environmental consciousnesses suitably raised. No doubt, she had added his name to a list of those in need of the most rigorous reeducation. After all, he lived on a *boat*, and everyone knew that boats, except for kayaks, paddleboards, and canoes were nothing short of being hazardous-materials sites.

I prayed daily for the fall rains.

I could have complained about the dogs to the marina office, but that would have only made things worse.

As a general rule, I keep myself to myself. Dick's a friend, but only just. According to me, Dick's my best friend from hell, and according to him, I'm nothing but a noxious dream.

Be that as it may, I didn't want to make trouble, and the dogs weren't specifically misbehaving. They were dogs behaving like dogs, yapping and pissing and snuffling.

Out of nowhere, Ralph asked, "Have you noticed those ropes hanging down into the water?"

"What ropes?" Dick and I asked at the same time.
"At first, I thought they could be crab-pot lines," Ralph said.
"But ... ?" Dick prompted.
"Well, I pulled one up, and there was nothing at the end of it but a frayed end. No crab pot."
"That's weird," I said.
"The line wasn't very long, either," Ralph added. "Couldn't have been attached to a crab pot."
Dick said, "They have to have some purpose."
"Yeah, but what?"
Matt Thurlow and his Golden Retriever, Digger, joined us. Matt had brought a deckchair, but no beer, which meant that he wasn't planning on staying for very long.
"Fuck it's hot," Matt said. "Muggy too."
We agreed that it was.
Then Matt asked, "You hear anything last night?"
"Like what?" Ralph asked.
"Like a dog crying."
"Crying?"
"Whimpering."
"No," Ralph said.
"Not a sound," Dick said, "but then I was out working most of the night."
I hadn't heard squat, so I kept quiet and looked on attentively.
"I must have been dreaming," Matt said.
"The heat will do that," Dick said.
"I guess."
"Maybe you ought to smoke a better grade of pot," Dick said.
"Who can afford the good stuff?"
"I would if I could, but I can't so I don't," Ralph said.

Dick glared at him, but covered it over with a relaxed smile that was about as relaxed as an overwound mainspring.

The two of them put on a good show, but a dark history existed between them, a feud, an animosity that had never quite subsided.

Whatever had caused the rift, it had happened long before I came along, thus I had no idea what it was, only that there was bad blood between them and that it refused to be stanched.

The conversation veered away from the price of pot and settled on accidents. Ralph told us about slamming his boat into a pump-out barge in a crosswind, and Matt told them about the time he'd gone aground up in Desolation Sound.

Dick said, "Shit, that's nothing. I was marooned on a desert island for a while. I was absolutely alone."

"How was it?" Matt asked.

"Crowded," Dick said.

Ralph looked as though he were going to drag out an old joke about voices, but we were spared, and he was saved from the embarrassment of having made it, by a loud splashing noise and a burst of doggy yelping from farther along the row.

The yelping cut off suddenly, but the splashing continued.

I recognized the yelp. Princess Pitti-Sing was at it yet again. That mutt was like an obnoxious 24-hour alarm service. If anyone walked by, if a seagull flew by, if a fish swam by, that batteries-not-included toy of a dog would start barking and yapping and wouldn't stop for at least ten minutes.

The noise, or rather, the splashing part of it, sounded like the same sort of splashing that we'd been hearing a lot lately, off and on, especially at night. We'd chalked it up to sea otters or seals or night-feeding birds.

MARINA DOGFISH CHOW

We ran toward the sound, arriving just in time to see a sea lion, a huge one, blackish-brown, making short work of Princess Pitti-Sing. She was a Pekingese cross. With what was impossible to tell. A Dachshund, maybe? Whatever the case, Princess Pitti-Sing was not pert as a puppy well could be.

Why "Pitti-Sing," a character from *The Mikado*, and why "Princess," apart from it being a term of endearment, were among the row's lesser mysteries.

The splashing was loud and violent.

The sea lion had clamped its jaws around the dog's middle and was shaking it back and forth, while simultaneously gulping down whatever hunks came loose. The dog was, mercifully, dead, or ought to have been dead by that point, but there remained on its face a mélange of shock, pain, and bewilderment.

Blood, viscera, hair, bone, muscles, and assorted oddments were spraying into the air and out across the water. They made little splashes where they landed. They looked like the splashes hailstones make when they hit a puddle. The dog's viscera were like mangled lengths of kelp that had turned pink.

Ralph said, "That's one hell of a coming out party."

Dick said, "Yep. She's been schooled, all right."

Matt said, "The joke's sure over for that one."

"I never liked that dog," Dick said. "Nice enough, but I never could warm up to her. Too much yapping."

"Face it, Dick, you hate dogs," Ralph said.

"I own a dog, genius," Dick said.

It appeared that the past was about to rear its ugly head.

"Now children," Matt said.

Ralph and Dick returned to their respective corners.

Meanwhile Cosmo and Hamish and Digger were fixedly

watching the drama in the water. For once in their lives they weren't pissing or barking or gobbling down treats.

I was convinced that Cosmo had bladder or kidney issues. No healthy dog could possibly pee that much.

By the time Princess Pitti-Sing's mommy and daddy crawled out of their gin bottles long enough to wonder what the commotion was all about, the sea lion had swum off. Inexplicably, it left behind a lingering, septic stench, as though it had brought its favorite haul-out spot with it.

The only thing left of Princess Pitti-Sing was her head. It was bobbing between two of the boats, a sketchy fly-bridge sedan that was rotting in her slip and a ten-year-old Jeanneau that may have gone out once in the last three years.

Mommy saw the head and began screaming at the top of her lungs.

Daddy looked blearily at the water but couldn't seem to focus. Gin will do that.

"What's that over there?" he asked, pointing at Pitti-Sing's head. "Somebody lose a cushion?"

The screaming redoubled.

~~*

ANOTHER EVENING, another round of beers. Matt Thurlow and Digger stopped by. This time, Matt brought his own beer, two bottles worth. He'd also brought a stainless-steel mixing bowl.

The dogs were suddenly beside themselves: tails wagging, eyes shining, jaws drooling.

Matt twisted the caps off both beers and, saving one for himself, poured the other into the bowl.

The dogs lunged at it.

Gulp, gulp, gulp, slurp, slurp, slurp, gulp, gulp, gulp ...

But they were responsible enough to pace themselves.

Having done so, Digger plopped his head down in Dick's lap. Ever the generous host, Dick scratched the dog's head.

I noticed that he was gritting his teeth, behind that same bland smile he liked to affect.

Matt said, "You guys hear anything funny last night?"

Dick said, "Oh, please! You sound like a broken record."

"Broken schmoken. Did you hear anything funny or not?" He sounded worried, worried to the point of anger. Not a good sign.

"I don't watch the news," Ralph said.

"Good one," I commented.

As though I hadn't said anything, Dick asked, "Funny ha-ha?"

"No, the other kind. Funny peculiar."

"What exactly did you hear?" Ralph asked. He sounded like a community-college teacher, the kind that suspects that teaching at a community college is a waste of his time and unparalleled expertise but who can't find a job teaching at a university.

"I couldn't stay asleep last night," Matt said. "I was awake at about two and I thought I heard some guy tromping down the walk, but quiet like, you know? And just like before, I heard a dog whimpering."

"Another dog?" Dick asked, skeptically.

"Yeah. Another dog," Matt said. "You know how they sound when they're scared?"

"Yeah," Dick said.

"I certainly do," Ralph said, his voice overly controlled.

Cosmo, Scotty, and Digger were all ears.

"Well, that's how it sounded. Terrified. Drugged, too."

"You mean like you did before you went in for your last lobotomy?" Dick asked. He was in fine form.

"Close enough, pencil prick."

"You're hearing things," Ralph said.

"Yeah, I must be," Matt said, and shook his head in mock despair. "Life sure can be a bitch when your brain's no better than hamburger."

Putting on his schoolmarm voice, Ralph said, "How many times have I told you to quit watching the news?"

"All I heard last night was that same old splashing," Dick said, cutting across Ralph's joke.

"When?" Matt asked, all seriousness.

"I got up to take a piss about three. That's when I heard it. Has to be otters. We've probably got a family of 'em living around here."

"I miss the old wooden docks," Ralph said. "The otters used to nest up between the stringers."

"Seals, too," Matt said.

Nobody mentioned the eye-watering stench of a seal rookery.

The conversation wandered around for a while, but then it landed on sharks.

Matt asked, "Are there sharks around here?"

Dick thought about it. "I don't see why not."

Ralph whipped out his smartphone. Tap, tap, tap. "We do," he said, and showed the screen to Matt. "Take a gander."

"I've never seen any," Dick said.

"Doesn't mean they aren't around," Ralph said, as though he'd played an ace of trumps.

"Sharks eat people, don't they?" Matt asked.

Dick and Ralph looked at him as though he were terminally naïve.

"Around here, though?" Matt said. "I've never heard of a shark attack in Puget Sound."

The smartphone came out again. Tap, tap, tap. "No unprovoked attacks in Puget Sound," Ralph announced.

"That's a relief," Matt said. "I don't have to give up paddle-boarding."

I cringed. Paddle-boarders and kayakers are the twin banes of the sailor's existence. Never mind that sailors are among the most avid paddle-boarders and kayakers on the water.

"Not hardly," Dick said. He swigged his beer. "What about dogfish?" he asked, making conversation. "They're all over and they're sharks, aren't they?"

"I guess," Ralph said.

Digger, Cosmo, and Scotty finished the beer in the bowl, and the party broke up.

On the way back to Ralph's boat, Cosmo pissed on Dick's hose bib.

Ralph apologized for his dog, but Dick told Ralph to, "Forget about it. It's not his fault."

"Dogs will be dogs," Ralph said.

"I hear you," Dick said, and went through the motions of hosing off his hose bib.

It was the politically smart move.

If he hadn't hosed off his fresh-water faucet, he would have been making a show of his unconcern, which, in a way, would have been worse than jumping up and down and yelling his head off, as in, "I'm fed up with your fucking mutt and his fucking piss!"

THE GREAT MYSTERY OF ETERNITY

As it was, Ralph went back to his boat.

To me, Dick said, "... and owners will be owners."

"That's true," I said.

Taking a chance, I asked, "Why haven't you moved to another marina? Come to that, why hasn't Ralph."

"Why would we do that?"

"Because you hate each other's guts."

"You noticed."

"Hard not to," I said. "Answer the question?"

"It's because neither one of us wants to be the one who's run out of Dodge."

"Fair enough, if it doesn't come to blows. Air horns at twenty paces, that sort of thing."

"It already has," Dick said.

"You're kidding!"

"Years ago. Over and done with."

"What over?"

"Stuff."

And with that, Dick went back aboard his boat, and life among the liveaboards went on as per usual.

~~*

LATER ON, at about two in the morning, when the night is at its darkest and the relief of the predawn remains a long way off, I heard the combination of sounds that Matt had asked us about: a stealthy tromping and a kind of chemically subdued, canine whimpering, not loud, but then I'm a light sleeper and have keen hearing. Maybe I should have been a security guard.

The sound tracked past my boat, past Dick's boat, past Ralph's boat, but stopped a little farther along the headwalk. As far as I could tell, the footfalls halted right about where *Lady of the Islands* was tied up.

Lady of the Islands was a Roughwater, complete with flying bridge and a dinghy mounted on her swim platform. She was a nice boat, but no one ever came near her. She had moss growing on her decks, and her various canvas covers—for her barbecue, anchor windless, and such—were literally rotting off.

After a time, the steps moved away, back the way they'd come, back on up the ramp.

The whining faded into silence.

I can't say how I knew, how I could be so certain, but I was absolutely convinced that the dog, that terrified, pathetic animal, was still there, tied to a mooring cleat. It had been left there, left to cower in *Lady of the Islands'* shadow.

But it was night, and the boat wouldn't have been casting a shadow. None. Not a speck. Apart from the black-on-black hints created by the safety lighting on the headwalk.

The silence and the dark.

Unbroken.

Complete.

Seemingly without end.

Staked out. Like a goat to bring in a tiger.

My clock chimed one bell: 4:30 in the morning.

Then came two bells: 5:00 A.M.

By this time the sky was lightening.

It brought no relief.

Its promise had been a lie.

People were making coffee and rummaging around for breakfast.

THE GREAT MYSTERY OF ETERNITY

They weren't the only ones.

I was downing my morning's first cup of coffee when I heard a yap, a growl, a bark, a watery rush, a terrified yelp, and then a second watery rush. The first rush had sounded like a swimmer breaking the surface after having stayed underwater for a long, long time, and the second rush had sounded like a diver plunging into the water from the side of a swimming pool.

I sprinted down to *Lady of the Islands*. I arrived with my shoes untied, my pants unzipped, and my sweatshirt on backwards.

The familiar, gluttonous maelstrom was taking place a few yards from the headwalk.

I couldn't see the dog, or what was left of it, and the sea lion was no better than a snout, eyes, and teeth, tearing at the carcass, blurs in the strengthening light.

The air stank of gutted dog.

The gulls swarmed in.

The sea lion disappeared, and gulls gulped down what they could.

Here and there, dogfish fins sliced through the water, leaving behind graceful V-shaped trails.

It was then that I looked down at my feet. I was standing in a puddle of water and blood.

Tied expertly to the nearest mooring cleat was a length of household clothesline. It wasn't the sort of rope you'd ever expect to find on a boat.

Dr. Chuck Davidson came off his boat, a 43' Hans Christian ketch, *China Doll*, moored outboard at the end of the row. Rumor had it that *China Doll* had been the "other woman" at the heart of Chuck's divorce.

From what I could gather, it had gone more or less like this:

"Chuck, it's either me or that smelly old boat!"

"Sorry you feel that way, Honeybunch. Good-bye."

His ex-wife, a high-end physical therapist, had come out of it with the house, the children, and Chuck's child-support payments. Chuck, a psychiatrist, had come out with making the mortgage payments, making the child-support payments, his boat, and his self-respect. All of which had been fine by him. They were his kids, and he was, thanks to a shrewd lawyer, building up a solid equity in the house.

He stopped and looked at the water where the sea lion had snagged its breakfast ... or part of it. Bits and pieces of the dog were drifting here and there, but the birds and the dogfish were avidly policing the water.

"The sea lion strikes again, eh, Doc?" I said.

Chuck didn't answer, but headed on up the headwalk toward the ramp.

For him, breakfast would be a quick tossed salad at a middle-grade restaurant and then he'd be off to work. For the rest of the working day, he'd listen to people bitch and whine, and occasionally he'd dispense pearls of direction. "Yes, of course I understand, Fred. You go on home now, take two of the alprazolam—no drinking, remember?—and call me in the morning." Or, "Maybe we ought to change your medication. How does that sound?"

It hadn't always been that way, but that's what it had turned into. Like his marriage.

He could leave his practice, like he'd left his marriage, but then where would the money come from? How would he make the child-support payments, the mortgage payments, the moorage payments, the yard payments? Good schools cost big money, houses don't pay for themselves, and bottom paint, even if he did the work himself, which he did, was only the beginning of the expenses.

The gate slammed closed, and the morning's quiet again settled over the marina.

The sea lion and Doc had taken their departures.

The dark was giving way to the light.

No fog, no rain.

The air was still, and I could smell the salt-smell of the Sound, mixed with the low-tide smell of the mud-choked sand.

The new day had arrived.

When things fell right, I ambled over to Dick's boat. He was making nice with his teak decks by installing new bungs. He'd already sanded the planks, or what are called planks, and was doing the bungs because he couldn't face pulling out the old Thiokol, cleaning the seams, and re-caulking them, which would, as it has been said, involve lots and lots of "Oh, glorious sanding."

Haimish, Dick's dog, was flaked out in the cockpit, in the shade of the boat's dodger.

"You hear anything last night?" I asked.

Without taking his eyes off what he was doing, Dick said, "That's a popular question these days."

"How about a popular answer."

"Okay, sport. I heard a sea lion about sunrise." He whacked an epoxied bung into place and wiped off the excess.

"No, not the sea lion. Earlier. In the wee hours."

"I was working last night," he said. He dabbed another bung into the epoxy and twisted it into the next hole. "Didn't get back until about four. Why? What did you hear?"

"Some clown tied a dog to one of the cleats. Down by *Lady of the Islands*. That's what the sea lion got. That dog."

Haimish looked up, ears cocked.

"You could have untied it," Dick said.

"Not my dog."

"What about your sense of compassion?"

"Sea lions need to eat, too," I said.

That was a prize-winning bullshit answer. I should have untied the dog and taken it to a shelter.

Dick glared at me. "You're afraid of dogs."

"I'm *leery* of dogs I don't know," I said. "Besides, maybe the guy who staked it out had a perfectly good reason for staking it out. Could be, couldn't it?"

"Nah, he's just a sick fuck."

"Never in a million years," I said. "What's he's doing is too complicated to be the work of a deranged mind."

"You haven't spent a whole lot of time around motels and boats, have you?"

Before I could answer, Ralph came over.

Cosmo trailed at his heels.

Ralph said to Dick, "Doc told me that that fucking sea lion that's been hanging around killed another dog."

"We don't know that it's the same one."

"You don't sound very surprised?"

"Should I be?"

Cosmo was peering down into the water.

I told Ralph, "You'd better keep your dog away from the edge."

Ignoring me, Ralph said to Dick, "Aren't you worried about Haimish?"

"Why? Should I be?" Dick said. An edge had crept into his

voice. It was almost as though he were accusing Ralph of feeding dogs to the sea lions.

Meanwhile, Cosmo was hanging over the water, neck stretched out, nose down, nostrils flaring.

I tried again. "I'm telling you, Ralph, you dog's gonna become dog chow if he keeps on poking his snout over the edge like that."

"I would be if Hamish were my dog," Ralph said, not paying the slightest attention to what I'd said. "Hell, I am worried about him. Have you talked to the office about what's going on?"

"Have you?" Dick said.

Neither of them had, of course. What happens on B Row stays on B Row ... or it goes to Las Vegas and stays there.

"I've heard of sea lions going after people," I said.

"What am I gonna tell 'em?" Ralph said.

As far as he was concerned, I might as well have not even been there.

"You could tell 'em about the sea lions, you dolt," I said. It never hurts to try.

Continuing to Dick, Ralph said, "I'd look like—"

Cutting Ralph off in mid-excuse, a dark brown sea lion about the size of a Clydesdale shot out of the water, snapped its jaws around Cosmo's neck, and pulled the dog off of the headwalk.

It happened so suddenly that Cosmo didn't get off so much as yip.

Then the sea lion dragged the dog through the gap between Dick's boat and the next one over and on out into the fairway. The dog left behind a splattered trail of blood. The dull red splashes on the gray-green-black water were like an avant-garde painting.

There, between the rows of slips the sea lion shook the dog

back and forth. Water flew in all directions, and in the midst of the splashes, the sea lion chowed down on the dog's viscera and other tasty morsels as they separated from the disintegrating mess than had been Ralph's treasured companion.

While this was going on, Ralph was, understandably, yelling and running back and forth like a wild man. "Who has a rifle? Shoot the bastard! Doesn't anybody have a fucking rifle?"

I had a 5-shot .38 with a 2-inch barrel, a relic of an earlier era, but at the moment, it would have been about as much use as a BB gun. I chose not to mention it.

Ralph's face was stop-sign red, his eyes were huge and bugging out of his head, and tears were running down his cheeks.

By this time, he was more or less shouting incoherently, and, too, by this time, fins were racing in toward the kill, toward the blood-scent and noise. Never to be left out, the gulls were diving and feasting on the sea lion's detritus.

Dick looked on impassively, but I imagined that I could detect a hint of satisfaction in the set of his face, in its rigid lack of expression. He wasn't about to race below and retrieve his .308 hunting rifle.

It was too late, much, much too late, anyway.

Pass out the black armbands, boys and girls. Let's drink a toast and remember Cosmo for the fine, loyal, and friendly, although remarkably stupid, pooch that he was.

I stood off to one side, out of the way. I'd tried to help before, to no avail, and there was nothing I could do now. There was nothing anyone could do, now that the sea lion had struck.

I could hear the chilling sound of Cosmo's bones snapping between the beast's jaws, like twigs being broken into kindling for a campfire.

THE GREAT MYSTERY OF ETERNITY

Then, as abruptly as it had begun, the attack ended. The sea lion dove away, and the dogfish and gulls moved in as never before. They scarfed down the last available bits of Cosmo's earthly remains. The gulls made more noise than the sea lion had. The dogfish made nearly none at all: now and then an energetic ripple, the susurration of fins powering through the water.

The mood on the headwalk turned on a dime.

"You're smiling!" Ralph railed at Dick. "You son of a bitch, you're actually smiling!"

"I am not," Dick said.

Doc strode up, looking out at the scene in the fairway.

"You're glad Cosmo's dead!" Ralph shouted.

Dick looked directly into Ralph's eyes. "No, I'm not."

"Cosmo?" Doc asked.

For a smart guy, he wasn't overly bright.

"Yeah," I said. "This time it was Cosmo's turn."

Doc asked Ralph, "Was it Cosmo?"

"That fucking sea lion took him right off the dock," Ralph said. Changing his focus, he pointed directly at Dick. "And he's glad about it."

Well, Cosmo had tended to piss on Dick's hose bib a lot. More than one would normally expect. Marking territory was one thing, but Cosmo had seemed to be sending a message.

"No, I'm not glad," Dick said.

Using his best psychiatrist expression, Doc said, "I know none of us would ever do such a thing, but someone has been using dogs as bait, to draw in the sea lions."

"What?" Dick demanded. "Are you nuts?"

"It's like attracting humming birds with humming-bird feeders," Doc said. "Whoever he is, he's training the sea lions to feed off the B-Row headwalk."

"Could be a she," I commented, in the spirit of gender equality. We had a few women, both wives and single gals, living aboard on B Row, not many but three or four. No, I tell a lie. We were down to three. Last year what's-her-face married a dentist from Poulsbo and sold her boat.

"Makes sense," Ralph said, glaring at Dick.

"Bull shit," Dick said. "Training sea lions? Come on, people. You don't have to train sea lions to chow down on whatever they can snag. They do it automatically."

His pitch wasn't finding any takers.

"Nevertheless ..." Doc said, in that tone of nonthreatening threat for which psychiatrists are infamous the world over.

"Okay. Fine," Dick said. "But staking out dogs to get eaten? Who'd do a sick thing like that?"

He was on his back foot now, although how he had ended up there, I had no idea. Dick? Outmaneuvered? Intimidated by a so-called mental-health professional? Never. Dick was more of an I'll-see-you-in-hell-first kind of guy.

Looking directly at Dick, our local psychiatrist said, "I can't say who he is, but he's seriously disturbed and needs professional help."

"I can say who he is," Ralph said. "But I won't."

The squawking and chittering of the gulls echoed across the marina.

~~*

NOTHING HAPPENED THAT NIGHT. It was too soon. However, the following night was another story.

THE GREAT MYSTERY OF ETERNITY

At about nine o'clock, Dick left on another one of his quasi-emergency calls. He was still gone at one in the morning. That's when I put on my darkest clothes, slipped my .38 into the pocket of my windbreaker, which was a stylish black, and went out onto the headwalk.

I was as good as invisible.

I went down to the end of the row, down by *China Doll*, found a handy spot next to a piling, and waited.

The scene had a surreal quality to it: the ineffective lighting, the marshmallow-shaped deck boxes, the neatly aligned bows, anchors almost but not quite extending over the headwalk, and the sterns, nearly touching that same headwalk, protected by fenders hanging over the trailing edges of the swim platforms.

Now and again, a heron would swoop from left to right or from right to left.

In the distance, over in the town, at random intervals, a motorcycle would scream through an intersection.

But mostly it was dark and quiet, another world, laced with the aroma of drying mud and saltwater.

At close to two in the morning, Ralph carried a gallon jug off his boat. From the way he hefted it, I could tell that it was full.

Before stepping out into the illumination on the headwalk, he looked carefully up and down.

He looked right at me, but he didn't see me.

No dog barked.

No startled bird put up a fuss.

Nothing and no one stirred.

Now certain that he was alone and unlikely to be seen, Ralph went over to Dick's hose bib and drenched it with some of the contents of the jug, perhaps two cups worth.

Then he moved to the next hose bib, and then to the one after that. He dribbled what could only have been his own urine onto the sides of two or three deck boxes, onto a half dozen more faucets, and onto several mooring cleats. Then he went back to Dick's boat, set the empty jug down, unzipped, and let fly, again dousing Dick's freshwater faucet.

I said nothing and I did nothing.

The .38 in my pocket was of about as much use as a T-bone steak in a vegan restaurant. What was I going to do with it? Bushwhack a man for playing a practical joke? For getting a little of his own back, or, rather, for acting on the assumption that he was? Not hardly. Call the cops and turn him in for littering? Double not hardly.

On the other hand ...

I couldn't do nothing. I couldn't allow him to drench our faucets with piss just because he thought Dick was using the local fauna to rid the row of its canines.

But if it wasn't Dick, then who was it? Matt? Doc? The drunk couple? I was as certain as I could be that it wasn't me.

While my alleged mind spun in circles I waited, not moving. I melded into the piling. I became a facet of the night, a shadow within the shadow-curtained darkness, a dream.

Ralph took his jug and went back aboard his boat.

Eventually, I returned to my own boat.

Good night, sweet Cosmo, may choirs of angels ...

~~*

I AWOKE with the idea fully formed.

Ralph was sure to repeat himself, sure to make sure that Dick realized what was happening.

Cosmo may be gone, but the pissing wasn't. Ralph was taking up where Cosmo had left off.

Good enough.

Then Ralph could learn what Cosmo would have learned if I hadn't dallied, if my nerve hadn't failed, and if the sea lion hadn't intervened.

Buying the parts, running the wires, and rigging Dick's hose bib wasn't child's play but it wasn't brain surgery, either.

With the nuts-and-bolts work completed, I had nothing left to do but wait, and wait is what I did.

One day.

Two days.

The marina was far from returning to normal, but the open rancor had gone into semi-hiding.

Doc and Ralph and Dick and I weren't joking and laughing, but neither were we hissing and clawing at one another.

Then, at 2:30 in the morning on the fourth day, Ralph unzipped, whipped it out, took aim, and pissed on Dick's faucet.

Down went Ralph's golden shower, down in a torrent of revenge.

However ...

He did not whoop and holler in triumph, nor in simple relief.

Instead, his body convulsed and he screamed in utter pain.

He threw himself backwards, away from the faucet, as though he were jerking his hand away from a hot stove, only it was his whole body. The last of his coordination gave out, or was overwhelmed, and he flopped down onto the float and lay there trembling and panting and whimpering and holding onto his crotch with both hands.

And with one leg dangling over the edge of the headwalk.

Like Princess Pitti-Sing, and like his own dog, Cosmo, he could have made a better choice.

"Get away from the edge, you jackass!" I yelled at him.

But he didn't respond.

Had the shock rendered him unconscious?

No, he was rocking back and forth, moaning and making a yeomanlike effort to recover himself.

God only knew how long it would take him to pee again with any degree of alacrity.

In an apparent effort to lever himself up onto all fours, he made the mistake of rolling closer to the edge.

"NO!" I shouted, but I was too late.

A sea lion, by far the largest I'd seen in the moorage, lunged up and grabbed Ralph's leg and dragged him kicking and screaming and thrashing into the water.

Ralph made an effort to clutch onto a mooring line, onto the bite itself, but despite his terror-charged efforts, his hands didn't have the strength to hold out, not for very long, against the enormous power of the sea lion.

Ralph's screams echoed across the marina, and lights came on up and down B Row.

There was a huge splash, and Ralph lost his grip, as I had known he would. He screamed. It was a panicked, horrified bawl, riddled with pain and confusion.

The sea lion dragged Ralph out into the fairway.

Ralph was thrashing and beating on the sea lion with his fists. Hammering on the monster's head, but to no avail.

The sea lion, it's grip on Ralph's leg absolutely solid, began to thrash his head back and forth, as though he were disemboweling a salmon. Or a dog.

Water and now arterial blood flew in high arcs above the fairway. I heard a bone snap and then a shriek of redoubled agony.

People came running.

They boarded boats in an effort to get as close to the struggle as possible, but there was nothing they could do, not really. One or two of them tried to lunge at the sea lion with extended boathooks, but, inevitably, they fell short.

Doc was trying to lower a hard-bottom dinghy, but, as he must have known deep down, by the time he could get it into the water and had rowed over close to the struggle, it would be all over for Ralph. Doc would have nothing to do but pick up whatever pieces had been left floating.

Dick was on the stern of his boat, with his rifle, but I could tell by the way he was handling it, aiming here, aiming there, his movements abrupt, he couldn't get a clear shot.

It said a lot for him that he was trying.

But Gary Pilsen, over on A Row, could get a clear shot, and he took it. The muzzle flash from his .30-06 lit up the night, and the report banged out over the water like a sharp clap of thunder.

The sea lion twisted as though it might have been hit and let go of Ralph's leg. The monster dove.

Ralph was no better than semi-coherent, barely aware of what was going on, but conscious enough to flail toward the nearest finger walk. His efforts were worse than feeble.

"You can make it, Ralph! Just a few feet to go!"

Life rings, lengths of rope, and floating cushions were thrown to him. Boathooks were extended toward him.

Luckily, as it turned out, no one jumped in to save him. Clearly, it would have helped in those circumstances. Someone could have tied a rope around his chest, if nothing else. Plenty of ladders were spaced along the docks, so climbing back out wouldn't have been a problem. Nevertheless, the safety training, the reluctance to make the problem worse by adding one more person to the problem, held.

"Not far now!"

The acid smell of the round Pilsen had fired traced between the boats, surprisingly pronounced in the night air.

"You can make it! Swim!"

Ralph was within reach of a boathook, mere feet from the tip of a finger walk, when the dogfish struck.

Ralph screamed, and we gasped and yelled and beat at the water with boat hooks.

The dorsal fins and tails churned the water as they took hunk after hunk out of Ralph's body. They were called dogfish, but they were, at root, sharks.

Ralph shrieked and shrieked, high-pitched, staccato outpourings of rages and agony. A red plume spread out around his jerking, convulsing body, and now, rather than smelling like a discharged round, the night smelled of blood and ruptured viscera.

People were willing to fight a sea lion or a shark, but not a whole school of them. They shrank back from the ends of the fingers and from the edges of the headwalk. They gaped in an emotion exceeding horror and revulsion, outrage and the sort of shock that reaches into the depths of the human soul.

They delighted in watching killer whales feed on salmon, in eagles stooping and making off with a fish, in wolves taking down a deer, but had they ever considered the proposition from the standpoint of the fish or the seal or the deer or ... the man?

Unobserved, unnoticed and unremarked, I quietly and stealthily removed the wiring from Dick's hose bib and secreted it away aboard my boat. I thought to let the main components sink, but decided against it. Sooner or later, we'd have divers searching across the muddy bottom.

~~*

BY THE TIME the police arrived, nothing but fragments were left of Ralph. A few of them had been collected in fishing nets, and others had been picked bodily from the water. Doc had snagged Ralph's head in an orange, building-supply bucket.

The expression frozen on Ralph's slashed and torn face, especially in his eyes, was beyond my feeble powers of comprehension, let alone description.

How had Louis XVI looked, staring up from the bottom of the basket?

The police took charge of the moorage's collection and added to it.

They took statements, but I closed myself in my boat, ignored their knocking, and thereby convinced them that I was not aboard. They moved on.

After all, how many times did they need to hear the story?

The divers searched and found a shoe, complete with Ralph's foot, already being attacked by crabs, a few shredded items of his clothing, his wallet, and part of his left arm.

It was dark again by the time the divers, the forensic technicians, and the police had taken down their yellow-and-black tape and gone away.

The night settled in, and I came out of hiding.

Dick's light was on, so I went over to his boat.

MARINA DOGFISH CHOW

He made coffees for us, splashed in generous amounts of single-malt, and we sat companionably and drank them.

The inside of his boat looked like the teak-lined study of a nineteenth century timber baron. In addition to the aromas of coffee and Scotch, it smelled subtly of teak oil, lemon oil, dishwashing soap, and a diesel engine that hadn't been run for several weeks.

I also caught a whiff of dog. Haimish was in his basket, under the dinette table, close to our feet, snoozing.

Dick and I talked about Ralph and Cosmo. We talked about Doc and Princess Pitti-Sing, a mutt that had never stopped yapping, and about the alcoholic couple who'd owned her. They were now buying their gin by the case, rather than by the bottle.

"I haven't seen Matt or Digger around," I said. "What's up with that?"

"Matt figured out that Digger is allergic to boats."

"That's kind of stupid."

"Not if you're Matt."

A shoe dropped. "Ah," I said. "Smart guy, Matt." I could only wait for the other shoe.

"Indeed he is. Out of sight, out of jaws."

"What about Haimish?"

"He's safe enough," Dick said. "I trained him to stay away from the edge ... and not to piss on water faucets."

The other shoe dropped. "You *trained* those sea lions!"

"No, I *trained* the dogfish!"

THE MOORING BUOY

Exploration by boat or ship often involves picking the best place the anchor. The prudent mariner chooses wisely.

CHARLES DE COURCY, PH.D., looked at the holograms of the mushroom-shaped object, and concluded that he might, just might get his old job back. The thought made him very happy.

His current job did not make him very happy. For one thing, his job was aboard the planetary survey ship *Plumper*, and for another, although he loved ships and boats in general, he had always despised survey ships, especially those of the maritime variety, of which *Plumper* was one. It was an inexplicable quirk, irrational, but there it was.

Plumper was currently plying the oceans and charting the islands of Barkley IV, an indisputably quasi-earthlike planet, currently under intense colonization. As for the *Plumper*, she and her two sister ships had been coaxed down from their construction orbit in pieces and assembled, hastily and not very expertly, on a patch of dry ground near the water's edge.

To put it mildly, there had been several such patches "up for grabs," as the captain had phrased it.

From there, the colonial authorities on-planet had completed and dispatched the ships.

De Courcy's office, where he was pouring over the image of the mushroom-shaped object, was a cold, damp, poorly lit cubbyhole down in the bowels of the ship. It smelled of curing paint and lubricating oil. The room's one bright spot was a holograph of his beloved sailboat, *Minerva*, a eleven-meter-long sloop. She was light, narrow, and fast.

Things didn't get any better when he wasn't working. His sleeping cabin, although located in "officer's country," was worse than his office. It was cold, damp, and poorly lit, too; however, there was no *Minerva* and thanks to the ship's atrocious ventilation system, the space reeked of tobacco smoke from the officer's lounge, cooking grease from the galley, and rancid garbage from countless places from the wardroom pantry to the crew's mess. The taste, as it were, of these delightful elements permeated everything: the food, the drinking water, and the air itself. Nothing was immune.

The ship's engines, generators, and pumps kept up a constant rumble and whine that rendered ordinary conversation a thing of the past. To make matters worse, the incessant vibration rattled the whole structure—the decks, the bulkheads, the doors, the hatches, the latches, the dogs, and even the lighting fixtures. It jostled coffee cups off of tables, and hurled them down onto steel decks, where, inevitably, they shattered. Miniature whitecaps blanketed the water standing in the toilet bowls.

In short, *Plumper* was an affront to the disciplines of naval architecture and marine engineering, not to mention esthetics and the creature comforts. She was not, as the saying goes, "a home and a feeder."

Moreover, the never-ending vibration, never mind the actual motion of the ship, played havoc with the fluid in De Courcy's inner ears—or so he maintained. The ship's surgeon said otherwise and suggested a mild antidepressant, which De Courcy refused to take.

No, it could not be said that the good ship *Plumper* made

THE MOORING BUOY

Charles De Courcy, Ph.D. feel one damn bit happy, and yet, apparently, she was destined to be the instrument by which he would drag his life back from the brink of professional oblivion.

Among the members of *Plumper*'s crew, De Courcy had the distinction of being the only exoarchaeologist. He also had the distinction of being the only member of the crew who had been, first, summarily removed from his *tenured* position at New Chicago University and, second, offered a survey job as a way of "possibly" worming his way back into academia and polite society.

De Courcy didn't give a shit about polite society, except to ridicule it, but he was, quite inexplicably, fond of the academic life. It had less than nothing to recommend it, was deadly dull, had all the charm of a cobra, and wasn't the least bit civilized, but he did love it so.

At the moment, as far as he was concerned, by official pronouncement, that life was a fond memory, light years away, but now, quite unexpectedly, it was within reach again, even, possibly, from a mud ball like Barkley IV. No, that was unfair. It was within reach precisely *because* of Barkley IV.

Among the habited worlds of the Stuart Sector, Barkley IV had the distinction of being the only one covered with more water than solid ground. In fact, it was eighty percent covered with water. The water was deep in places, but for the most part, it was no more than five hundred meters deep. Most of it was less than a hundred meters deep. Thirty and seventy-five meter readings were common.

The twenty percent of the planet that was land, or what passed for land, was grouped into several low-lying archipelagos: rocks, islets, and islands. There was nothing the size of a continent anywhere on the planet. The highest elevation was 237.56 meters.

There was no evidence of sentient life, that is to say, life that was as sentient as human beings, if one could, in all candor, call human beings sentient, in the first place. De Courcy doubted it. That was what made universities such enjoyable places—all that intellectual might with nothing to do but envy and scheme.

Speaking of which ...

De Courcy commed the bridge. He made his report to the officer of the watch, repeated it to the first officer, repeated it again to the captain, repeated it yet again to the colonial authorities on-planet, who told them to stand by.

The engine note dropped and the ship slowed to a stop. She fell off broadside to the wind, and rolled on the swell. The vibration did not stop, but now the rhythmic clink and thunk of loose objects, shifting as the ship rolled sickeningly, was added as an undernote to the general din.

The captain called him to the bridge. From there, the two of them went into her day cabin. She brought up the image that had caused all the fuss. "Ok, Chuck, what is it?"

She delighted in calling him Chuck. She was always Captain, or Captain Moresby, or ma'am, but never Virginia.

"I'm an archaeologist, not a clairvoyant," De Courcy said.

"Guess."

"I'd say it looks like a mushroom anchor that's dug itself way into the bottom."

"How do you know what a mushroom anchor looks like?"

He told her about *Minerva* and about the mooring buoy he had set for her in Cortes Bay, garden spot of Victoria Sound, a mooring buoy held in place by a mushroom anchor.

"I'm happy for you," she said, with a dollop more sarcasm

than was needed. "Seriously, though, it can't be. A mushroom anchor? Out here in the middle of nowhere?"

"I said it *looks* like a mushroom anchor. I didn't say it *is* a mushroom anchor."

She gave him her Number One Skeptical Look. It was part grin, part disbelief, and part stoicism. "Okay, I'll play along. If it is a mushroom anchor, then whose is it?"

Whose? was right. So far, Barkley IV had yielded no sign of indigenous habitation, either currently or in the past. As far as any of the survey crew could tell, the planet was an absolute wilderness, apart from the half dozen colonial settlements that had started up: mining, refining, farming, manufacturing, more farming, and a resort complex complete with a marina. If nothing else, the planet was a sailor's paradise, an almost perfect combination of warm weather, open oceans, sheltered cruising grounds, and quiet anchorages.

De Courcy was almost sorry he hadn't brought *Minerva*. They wouldn't have let him, and she was better off in storage, but that didn't mean he didn't regret not having her. On the other hand, maybe he and his boat were better off letting some other poor, dumb schlub be the first to discover the hard way that the water was filled with single-celled organisms that loved to burrow into glass reinforced plastic like so many microscopic teredo worms. Not that there were any such organisms. As far as anyone knew.

"Why don't we find out what it is *before* we start worrying about who left it there."

Moresby glared at him.

"The *what* will give us the *who*, anyway," she said.

As an archaeologist, let alone and exoarchaeologist, De Courcy knew what a hoot that was, but he let it go. "No doubt," he said. He did not add, If you expand your determination of *what* far enough.

There was a polite rap on the door.

"Come," Moresby said.

The first officer poked his head into the room. "Colonial's on the blower for you, ma'am."

"Thanks, Bohai." To De Courcy, she added, "You're with me."

What more could a guy ask for?

The upshot of the exchange with Colonial was that based on an analysis of the image and other data provided, the boffins had determined that the object was not natural but was indeed an artifact.

De Courcy could almost feel the cold, crisp campus mornings in the fall, taste the unparalleled cinnamon rolls in the faculty-only lounge, inhale the delicious, heady scent of the library. Yes, Dr. De Courcy. No, Dr. De Courcy. Will that be all for now, Dr. De Courcy?

Therefore, the planetary governor, no less, was instructing *Plumper* to drop whatever she was doing at the moment and "to take whatever steps might prove to be necessary to determine the nature and origin of the artifact and to return with it to Colonial headquarters as soon as possible."

The publications, the books, the lecture tours, the polite jealousy of his colleagues. The money. The new roadster. The new sails for *Minerva*. The new autopilot. The new electronics. The new paint. The consulting fees. The exquisite vindication. With never a gloating words said. And never an I-told-you-so for him. It would be so much better that way. Served cold.

Captain Moresby acknowledged her instructions with the required hint of dutiful groveling.

Rather than breaking the link, the colonial bureaucrat asked, "Have you heard from *Discovery* in the past forty-eight hours?"

Moresby's face registered as much surprise as she dared. "I'll check the comm logs, but I don't believe we have, sir. Is anything wrong?"

"She's overdue with her daily reports. We thought you might have picked something up."

"Sorry, sir, but we haven't. Is there anything we can do?"

"Keep your ears on," he said. "Relay any messages from her. Check your logs."

Moresby checked the logs. Nothing. Not a peep out of *Discovery* in the last two days. Moresby reported it.

Meanwhile, *Plumper* returned to the area where her scanners had detected the artifact, and came to a complete stop, holding her position with bow and stern thrusters. She was outside the entrance of a long, narrow bay, sheltered behind a natural breakwater. According to the scanners the bottom inside was fine-grained sand. A horseshoe-shaped run of wooded hills bordered the bay. De Courcy thought that he had never seen such a beautiful natural anchorage.

Remote scanners were deployed.

They spluttered and gurgled into the bay and were soon sending back streams of data, plus images of the artifact.

Moresby launched an aerial reconnaissance drone.

To her, De Courcy said, "Does this mean you believe me?"

"No, it means I'm doing my job," she said. Relenting a fraction, she added, "Whatever it is, it sure as hell isn't a Navy stockless."

An hour later, they had a working chart of the area. The bay was two kilometers long and a half kilometer wide. It was between twenty and twenty-five meters deep right up to the shoreline, with a mud-and-sand bottom and little weed.

It was too perfect, as though it had been dredged out of the island, scoured of excess weed and grass.

The artifact lay far down in the mud in the exact center of the bay. On the floor of the bay, however, right above the anchor was a rounded hump about the size of a lifeboat. It was a trifle odd, the coincidence of it being right there, but in and of itself, it wasn't the least bit unusual. Sand moved, formed hillocks, below the surface and well as on dry land.

"Hazards, Bohai?" Moresby asked the first officer.

"None that I can see," Bohai said. "No rocks. No snags. We can go in if you want to."

Moresby commed Colonial.

The colonial bureaucrat told her that it was her show.

Then he said, "We've learned that *Discovery* sank."

De Courcy felt his stomach tighten. It was as though he were two people: one whose stomach was clenching and a second one who was taking in the show from a safe distance.

Moresby's face went blank. "Survivors?"

"None."

Moresby's face hardened. "What happen?"

The ship filled up with water, De Courcy thought, but did not say so out loud.

"We don't know yet, but we do know that whatever it was, it was quick. We've sent *Resolution* to investigate."

Of course it had been quick; otherwise, *Discovery* would have sent a distress call and there would have been no mystery, no forty-eight-hour gap in her stream of daily reports.

"Understood," Moresby said.

She went to the bridge and conned the ship into the bay.

The turn around the end of the natural breakwater was tight, but the water was deep, no current to speak of, and Moresby made it look easy. Maneuvering at dead slow, she relied on the ship's twin screws alone, making no use of either the ship's bow or stern thrusters.

It was as pretty a piece of ship handling as De Courcy had ever seen, and his estimation of his gallant captain went up by several notches.

Once inside the bay, Moresby proceeded for a spot over the artifact.

When *Plumper* was two hundred meters off, a mass of bubbles erupted from the surface of the water over the artifact. The bubbles grew into a froth, and a moment later, a large, blue-and-white sphere popped to the surface. A heavy ring stood upright on top of it. The circumference and the upper surface of the sphere was covered with symbols.

Moresby and her bridge crew stared at it, silently, openmouthed.

Moresby was the first to recover her wits. "All back," she ordered.

"All back," came the reply. Then, "Engines answer all back."

"Very well."

Just as the ship came to a stop, Moresby said, "All stop."

"All stop." Then, "Engines answer all stop."

"Very well."

De Courcy snatched up a pair of binoculars and stared at the blue-and-white sphere. "It's a mooring buoy," he said. "Has to be. Only thing it can be."

"Maybe," Moresby said, settling and resettling her own pair of binoculars. "We don't know what it is."

"I think we should pick it up," De Courcy said.

"As in tie up to it?" the first officer asked.

"Exactly."

"It has writing on it, or something that looks a lot like writing," Moresby said. "Can you read it, Chuck?"

"No, of course I can't," De Courcy said.

"Then, assuming that it is a buoy, we can't tell whether it's a mooring buoy or an aid to navigation. For all we know, it could be marking a hazard, or it could be a quarantine buoy, or restricted, or some other sort of buoy."

"Yeah," De Courcy said. He had nothing else to say. She was right. They didn't know what it was. For sure. On the other hand, that ring made it pretty clear. After all, the more Earthlike planets that were discovered, the more universal certain things proved to be. Skies on planets with oxygen-nitrogen atmospheres tended to be blue—of one shade or another—because sunshine diffused through oxygen-nitrogen atmospheres in pretty much the same way regardless of what the planet was called. And so it went.

A mooring buoy was likely to look like a mooring buoy no matter where it was because that particular configuration was efficient and useful.

"Look, Captain, you're right. We can't tell for absolute certain, but I still think we'd be wise to tie up to it."

"Nothing doing," Moresby said, and began the maneuvers required to anchor the ship.

The instant the hook was down, long before it dug into the bottom, the buoy turned from blue and white to green and black, and sent up an ear-splitting howling. Lights emerged from inside the sphere and flashed.

"That's done it," De Courcy said.

"Done what?" Moresby asked.

"*It*. How should I know which *it*?"

"You're the exoarchaeologist."

"Yes, but I'm not an oracle."

"Captain," the first officer called. He was standing farther out along the bridge wing. "We have a problem."

They rushed to look over the side.

Around the ship the water was beginning to boil. It reminded De Courcy of holovideos he'd seen of a school of piranha devouring a tapir. Maybe it had been a tapir. It could have been a wild pig. No matter what it had been, it had ended up a skeleton in a matter of seconds.

It was then that De Courcy heard the new sound. It wasn't the sound of engines, or generators, or pumps, or ventilation fans. It was the sound of metal being ripped apart. The sound of tiny metal teeth cutting into the ship, devouring it.

The reports began coming in.

Flooding.

Bulkheads giving way.

Crewmen swarmed over and reduced to pulp, the pulp reduced to pink smears in the water.

Equipment failures.

Moresby ordered the anchor raised. The chain came up, but the anchor was missing. The last link looked as though it had been cut through with a dull hacksaw.

She ordered the engines ahead full. The shafts raced, but the ship did not move. The propellers were gone.

Plumper began to settle. She went down by the head first,

then took on a slight starboard list.

"Engine room's flooding, ma'am," the first officer reported.

A look of defeat and unexpected horror filled Moresby's face.

The engines stopped. The pumps stopped. The generators stopped. The lights went out. The lights came back on, now running off the backup batteries. The ventilators stopped. The ship was utterly quiet. Except for the sound of those trillions upon trillions of gnawing, devouring teeth.

The lights went out.

The batteries were gone.

Over and above the grinding of those teeth came the screams of the crew below decks. Rushing to get out. Finding their paths blocked by collapsing structures, by jammed door. By darkness. By their own panic. By the multiplying red smears in the water rising around their ankles, around their knees, around their waists. Ripping them apart. Consuming them alive.

"Abandon ship!" Moresby ordered, yelling the words. "Pass the word, abandon ship!"

She ran from the bridge wing. "You're with me, Doc," she called over her shoulder.

Doc. Better than Chuck. Much better.

De Courcy followed at her heels.

She raced into the comm shack. A terror-stricken operator sat at his machines, hysterically frozen.

"We have to broadcast a mayday," Moresby said, shoving him out of the way.

"Using what for electricity?" De Courcy said.

"The comms have their own power," Moresby said. "Batteries."

The bulkheads were covered with an advancing, seething

mass. De Courcy recognized them for what they were: nanobots. So it seemed that humanity wasn't the only sentient race to invent the little darlings. As inevitable as fire and agriculture. Given the right conditions. Given enough time.

They were slithering toward the helpless operator.

The Colonial bureaucrat's face appeared on one of the screens.

"Virginia? Is that you?" he asked.

"We're under attack."

"I called to warned you. Whatever you do, don't drop anchor anywhere near anything that looks like a mooring buoy."

"You're a little late with the warning, Frank," she said.

For De Courcy, the pieces fell into place—click, click, clank. The idyllic planet. The utter lack of habitation. The disguised automatic buoy. Probably one of countless thousands scattered around. He'd been right. Dropping anchor had been a first-class no-no. There were coral reefs like that back home. They'd been free to tie up, but not to anchor.

Discovery before them and now *Plumper* had stumbled into the equivalent of another culture's wilderness area, one that that other culture valued very highly, more highly than most humans could possibly imagine.

And now *Plumper*'s crew was paying the price.

No doubt the retribution would spread.

Moresby screamed and went down, covered in a writhing mass of nanobots.

De Courcy felt the ship shift under him, felt her begin to roll onto her side and settle in the thirty-meter-deep water.

He felt the shudder of her bow striking the bottom, felt the continued roll, felt the water sloshing around his legs. He tried to move, to flee the comm shack, but he couldn't get his legs to move, his hands to drag him out. Like the operator, De Courcy's terror had frozen him in place.

His skin tingled. He dared not look for fear of what he would see. And then his skin burned, the pain intensified into a scream that filled his mind, the flooding compartment.

The ship went onto her side, throwing him against a bulkhead, stunning him.

Utter darkness.

Utter pain.

He was being eaten alive. Like the tapir. Or the wild pig.

He would have preferred to drown, but he didn't have that much time left.

A sudden bubble of calm opened.

He thought of the university, of the book deals, the lecture tours, the money, the new car, the new sails for *Minerva*.

He was glad that he hadn't brought her. She deserved better.

REVIEW AND CONTACT

If you enjoyed this story and would like to encourage others to read it, please take a moment to review it.

If you would like to receive notices of Jamie McNabb's blog posts, future publications, and special promotions, please sign up for his email list. Here's the link:

http://eepurl.com/ciisfb

Your comments and/or questions are important. If you would like to contact Jamie McNabb, here's the link:

http://bit.ly/2Ii9y49

ABOUT THE AUTHOR

Jamie McNabb writes in several genres.

His short fiction appears in a variety of print, online publications, and through Soapbox Rising Press.

His website is

> http://www.jamiemcnabb.com

If you would like to receive notices of Jamie McNabb's blog posts, future publications, and special promotions, please sign up for his mail list. He promises not to send spam, and you can opt out at any time. Here's the link:

> http://eepurl.com/ciisfb

CPSIA information can be obtained
at www.ICGtesting.com
Printed in the USA
FSHW010342030121
77341FS